Deadly Moves

From the Tales of Dan Coast

Deadly Moves

From the Tales of Dan Coast

By

Rodney Riesel

Published by Island Holiday Publishing
East Greenbush, NY

ISBN: 978-0-9971149-4-2

First Edition

Special thanks to:

Pamela Guerriere

Kevin Cook

Cover Design & Maps by:

Connie Fitsik

Cover Photo Copyright:

www.123rf.com/profile_chaoss'>chaoss /123RF Stock Photo

To learn about my other books friend me at

https://www.facebook.com/rodneyriesel

For Brenda,
Kayleigh, Ethan
& Peyton

KEY LARGO

ISLAMORADA

MARATHON

BIG PINE KEY &
THE LOWER KEYS

KEY WEST

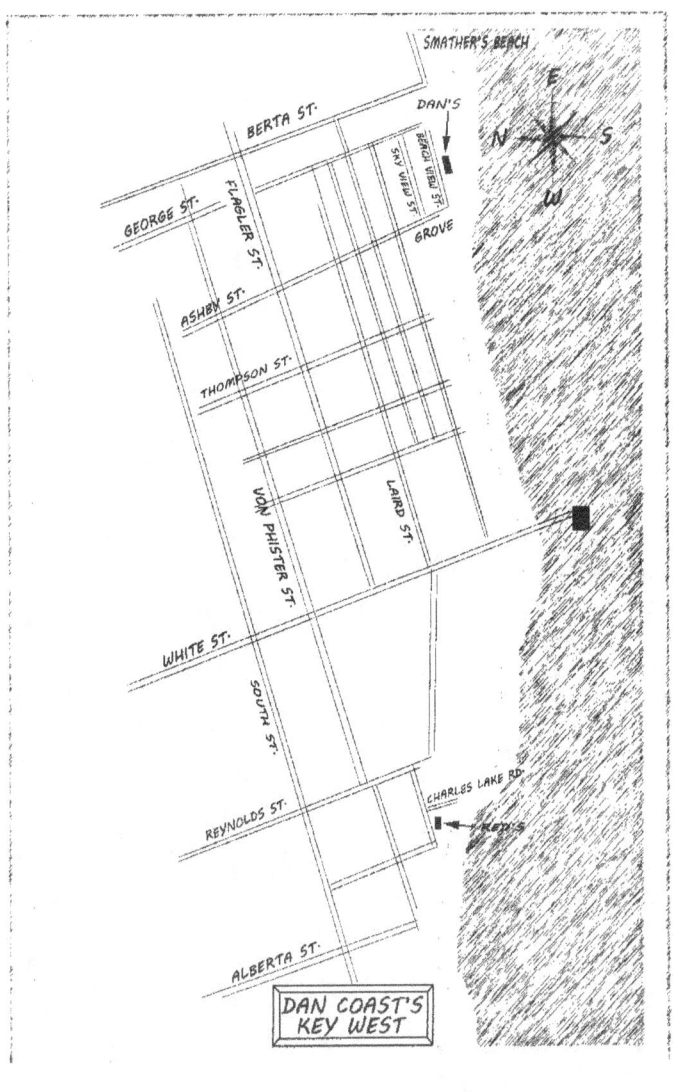

SMATHER'S BEACH

BERTA ST.

DAN'S

BEACH VIEW ST.

SKY VIEW ST.

GEORGE ST.

FLAGLER ST.

GROVE

ASHBY ST.

THOMPSON ST.

LAIRD ST.

VON PHISTER ST.

WHITE ST.

SOUTH ST.

CHARLES LAKE RD.

REYNOLDS ST.

KEN'S

ALBERTA ST.

N E S W

DAN COAST'S
KEY WEST

Chapter One

Dan Coast sat at one of the round four tops at Red's Bar and Grill. Across from him sat Ryan Jenkins. To Dan's right was the front door; Mel Gormin was sitting on his left.

Mel had recently grown a mustache in emulation of his current TV hero, Thomas Magnum, and was wearing a red Hawaiian shirt and faded blue jeans. Hanging around his neck by a thin piece of yarn was his aluminum foil-covered cardboard badge; a Detroit Tigers baseball cap decorated his head.

The jukebox was quietly playing "Chicken Fried" by the Zac Brown Band. It was three in the afternoon and the last of the lunch crowd had just walked out the door.

"I didn't know you had a partner, Coast," Jenkins said. Half a bottle of Landshark lager sat on the table in front of him.

Dan glanced over at Mel and then back at Jenkins. "I don't have a partner. He's just a friend."

"Best friends," Mel corrected. "When he has a tough case he usually asks for my help."

"Was my case a tough one?" Jenkins asked.

"No," Dan responded.

"So what did you find out?"

"Nothing."

"Nothing?"

"No. There's no evidence at all that your wife is cheating on you. I followed her every day for three weeks, Jenkins. Three mornings a week she goes to the gym. A couple mornings a week she runs and does yoga in the back yard while she listens to some godawful hip-hop music."

"She has a fantastic body," Mel said matter-of-factly.

"Thank you," said Jenkins.

"I followed her to the grocery store a few times," Dan said. "I wandered around Kmart a few times, too. I never even saw her *speak* to another man. Even at her tennis lesson, her instructor never touched her. She never did one thing even remotely suspicious. I don't know what you were so worried about."

Jenkins slumped back in his chair and sipped his beer. "Huh."

"You sound almost disappointed," Dan observed.

"Yeah, well, what are ya gonna do?" said Jenkins. He grabbed his beer by the neck and took a quick swig. Some suds leaked out from the corners of his mouth; he wiped it away with the back of his hand.

"Her not cheating on you is a good thing, Jenkins," Dan reminded him.

"Not in my case."

"Okay, what's going on here?" Dan asked. "I tell you your wife is faithful and you look like you just got the worst news ever."

"I want out of this marriage, Coast. We signed a prenup. If I divorce her she gets half of everything … unless she's unfaithful, then she gets nothing."

"Can I get you guys another drink?" Red called out from behind the bar. He was polishing glasses and stacking them on a shelf behind the bar.

"I'll have an Old Dusseldorf in a longneck," Mel said.

"He'll have a water," Dan corrected.

Mel shot him a dirty look.

"So you were *hoping* I would find out she was *having* an affair." Dan surmised.

"Of course. What am I gonna do now?" Jenkins asked.

"If you would like, I can sleep with your wife," Mel offered. "It would solve your problem."

Jenkins seemed intrigued. "How would you go about that?" he asked.

"Oh, don't worry, the ladies love me. I could have her in the sack within three day, tops. One if she has daddy issues."

Jenkins cocked his head. "That might just be crazy enough to work."

"No, it wouldn't!" Dan shouted. "You're not going to pay me to have Mel sleep with your wife. That would make me his pimp, for Chrissakes."

"You're right, it's probably a stupid idea," Jenkins agreed. "I'll just give the money to Mel, directly."

"There's no probably about it," Dan explained. "It is a stupid idea. Maybe you should look into some marriage counseling. Maybe you can work things out."

"That would just make things worse," Jenkins explained. "I told my girlfriend I would be divorced by the end of the year. She's getting pretty impatient."

"You have a girlfriend?" Dan asked judgmentally.

"There's nothing in the prenup about *me* having an affair."

"Oh, what's your girlfriend's name?" Mel asked.

"Bunny."

"Is she as hot as your wife?"

"Heavens no."

"Well then, eh—"

"What the Christ?" Dan shouted. "I can't help you, Jenkins. I did what you asked. Now, give me the rest of my money and we'll go our separate ways."

Jenkins reached into his back pocket. "Is a check okay?"

"Cash," Dan replied.

"Um, Dan," said Mel.

"Yeah, Mel, what is it?"

"The hot yoga lady is pointing a gun at us."

Everyone's head turned toward the door. Jenkins' wife was holding a .38 revolver. Her arm was straight and the pistol was turned to the side. It was obvious she had never held a gun before and her weapons training had come from any number of gangbangers on any number of cop shows.

"What are you doing, Margo?" Jenkins voice was shaking.

12

"So, you thought I wouldn't find out, you bastard!" Margo shouted. Her hand was shaking. She pulled the hammer back. Everyone in the room could hear it click into place.

Dan looked toward the bar out of the corner of his eye. Red was gone. He had dropped down behind the bar and taken cover.

"Margo, put the gun down," her husband pleaded.

Mel stood. "Ma'am, lower the gu—"

Margo pulled the trigger. Everyone flinched. The bullet passed between Dan and Mel, and hit the wall behind them. Margo cocked the gun again.

Mel quickly returned to his seat. "Sorry, ma'am."

"It's that whore that cuts your hair, isn't it?" Margo yelled.

"Is it the whore that cuts your hair?" Mel whispered.

"Yes," Jenkins whispered back.

Mel shouted, "He said it is her. It is the whore that cuts his hair!"

Margo aimed the weapon and fired, hitting Jenkins in the shoulder.

Dan flipped the table on its side and took cover.

Red jumped up from behind the bar and hurled a full bottle of Dos Manos tequila at Margo. Margo never saw the bottle coming. It hit her square in the forehead, dropping her to the floor in a pile of scorned woman. The bottle shattered on the floor next to her.

Jenkins lay next to the table, white as a sheet. "Somebody call an ambulance!" he yelled hoarsely.

Red was already punching 911 into his cell phone.

Dan stood and looked down at Jenkins. "Is there anything in the prenup about attempted murder?"

"No, but this just might be enough to get me out of this marriage." Jenkins' head fell back on the floor; he was out cold.

Mel was still seated in his chair. "Wow," he said. "This place is crazier than the nut house."

Chapter Two

Maxine Myers stood at the screen door overlooking Dan's backyard. She held two plates of scrambled eggs, bacon, and toast. She pushed the door open with her knee and walked down the gravel path that led to the two Adirondack chairs next to the fire pit.

Mel Gormin sat in one chair reading the financial section of the Key West Citizen. Dan Coast sat in the other chair reading the funnies. Dan's arms were extended in front of him, holding the newspaper as far away from his face as he could get it.

"Looks like someone needs glasses," Maxine observed.

"Looks like someone just needs longer arms," Dan corrected. "The way they print these goddamn newspapers nowadays it's hard to believe *anyone* can read them. Small print, blurry letters, next thing you know they'll start printing the news on black paper."

The reading glasses debate had gone on for months now. Maxine really began applying pressure when she noticed one afternoon how greasy Dan's hair had become. It only took Maxine a few days to determine that Dan could no longer read the shampoo bottles in the shower. For weeks he had been washing his hair with conditioner, rinsing, and then conditioning his hair with conditioner. Of course, Dan blamed Maxine because until she showed up there had been only one two dollar jug of coconut scented shampoo in the bathroom, and not one bottle of conditioner. Maxine made Dan an eye appointment the following Monday morning—an appointment that he never showed up for.

Maxine handed Mel his plate and then Dan's to him. "Yeah, I would imagine it's the newspaper."

"I don't think it's the newspaper," Mel informed them. "I can read it just fine. You probably should have your eyes checked."

Dan shot Mel a look. "I should probably have my *head* checked for bringing you here."

"I'm just saying, maybe glasses would help."

"I'll make you a deal. I'll get my eyes checked and then we'll get you fitted for a muzzle."

"I've never bitten anyone," Mel argued.

"You're right. We'll use duct tape instead."

"Am I gonna have to separate you two boys?" Maxine scolded.

All three turned to look when they heard Bev's screen door slam. Bev, holding a cup of coffee, walked onto her deck, down the steps, and across her backyard toward the group. Buddy, who had been lying on Bev's deck in the sun jumped up and followed close behind her.

"Morning, neighbors," Bev said.

"Morning," they all responded.

Mel jumped up. "Here, beautiful Bev, take my seat. I'll grab a lawn chair out of the shed."

"Thank you, Mel," said Bev, taking a seat in the Adirondack chair. She glanced at Dan and added, "Nice to see that chivalry isn't completely dead." Dan managed a grunt.

"Can I make you something for breakfast?" Maxine asked. "There's more bacon in there, and I can throw on a couple eggs."

"No, thanks, Maxine. I've already eaten."

"Where's Kip this morning?" Dan asked.

"He didn't stay over last night," Bev replied.

"Everything okay?" Maxine asked.

Mel returned with a lawn chair, unfolded it and set it next to Bev. He took a seat and rested his plate on his knee.

"I guess," Bev responded. "We broke up last night."

"What did you do?" Dan asked.

"What makes you think *I* did something?"

"Well, I can't imagine Kip Larson did anything wrong."

"Why?" Maxine asked. "Because he's your childhood hero who walked on the moon?"

"He never walked on the moon," Dan informed her.

"No one did anything wrong," Bev assured him. "We just decided that it wasn't meant to be."

"Wasn't meant to be," Dan repeated. "How could it not be meant to be? He's an American hero."

"Just like GI Joe," Mel added.

"What are we gonna do now?" Dan asked.

"We?" Bev asked.

"Am I still gonna see him? What happens now?"

"We'll find that out at the custody hearing," Bev answered sarcastically. "Maybe he can get you on the weekends."

"Very funny," Dan said. "This is so depressing."

"I realize you're hurt," Bev said. "but you have to understand, this wasn't your fault and we both still love you."

"Okay, okay, that's enough." Just then Dan's cell phone rang, he pulled it from his pocket. "Hello?"

"Dan Coast?" a man asked.

"That's me."

"My name is Preston Harvey. I was referred to you by Joseph Pantucco."

"And?"

"And me and a client I manage will be in Key West for a week starting Thursday. We will be staying at the Atlantic Inn. I'm looking for someone to work security."

"Security? What do you mean by security?"

"My client is in the film industry, Mr. Coast. I need someone to be with her whenever she goes out. You know, keep away the paparazzi, things like that."

"A bodyguard."

"Yes. Is that something you do, Mr. Coast?" Preston asked.

Without hesitation, Dan replied, "Yes, all the time. I do that quite a bit. I'm a security expert for Chrissakes."

Maxine, Bev, and Mel all cocked their heads and gave him a confused look.

"Excellent," said Preston. "Our plane will be arriving Thursday afternoon at 1:45. If you can give me your email address I'll send you all the information as well as Ms. Hunt's itinerary for the week."

Dan thought quickly. "Um … my email is down at the moment."

"Down?"

"Yeah, uh … somebody hacked it. I'll call you back in about a half hour and give you my email. It should be back up and running by then."

"Okay. I look forward to hearing back from you."

Dan hung up his phone.

"Your email was hacked?" Maxine asked.

"You're a security expert?" Bev asked.

"Can I have more bacon?" Mel asked.

Dan tossed his phone to Maxine. "Can you set me up an email account, please?"

Maxine snatched the phone out of the air and began tapping buttons.

"Who are you going to be body-guarding?" Bev asked.

"Some movie star."

"Name?"

"He just said her last name was Hunt."

"It's a woman?" Maxine asked.

"Oh, what if it's Helen Hunt!" Bev said. "I really like her."

Maxine finished setting up the email and tossed the phone back to Dan. "Your email address is dancoastkeywest@gmail.com, and your password is buddythedog123."

"Awesome," Dan said, and dialed the phone.

"The P Harvey Agency, Preston speaking."

"Hey Preston, it's Dan Coast. My email address is dancoastkeywest@gmail.com, and my password is buddythedog123."

"Okay. Thanks Mr. Coast, I'll send that information out toot sweet."

Dan hit the end call icon. "He's sending the information toot sweet."

"Toot sweet?" Bev asked.

"That's what he said."

Maxine held out her hand. "Give me your phone."

"Why?"

"So I can change your password. Don't tell people your password; only you have to know that."

"Oh," Dan replied, tossing her the phone.

Mel sat silently for a few seconds and then asked, "Can I get some more bacon, toot sweet?"

Chapter Three

"I don't know why I have to ride in the backseat," Dan stated as they drove along Flagler Avenue.

"You know Mel can't ride in the backseat," Maxine said. She took a left onto South Roosevelt Boulevard.

Mel gave Dan a big grin. "Yeah, Dan. I get car sick. Remember?"

"You're probably just making that up so you can ride shotgun and I gotta sit back here."

"Dan, you know I would trade places with you if I could," Mel said unconvincingly.

"Whatever," Dan replied.

Maxine turned right onto A1A. "Where is this place again?" she asked.

Dan pulled a piece of folded paper from the front pocket of his cargo shorts and unfolded it. He read his notes aloud. "Take a right on Cross Street, go to the end, and take a left on Twelfth Avenue."

Maxine followed the directions and pulled to the curb in front of a peach-colored, one story block home.

"That must be the car there under the tarp," Dan surmised.

The three climbed out of the car and walked through the white wrought iron gate in the block fence that surrounded the property. As they got to the car the front door opened.

"Can I help you?" asked a tall, thin man Dan judged to be in his late fifties.

Dan pointed toward the car. "I'm Dan Coast, I called yesterday about buying the car."

"Oh, yeah, Mr. Coast. I've been expecting you."

Dan approached the man with his hand extended.

"Mitch Fallon," the man said and shook Dan's hand. "That's her right over there under the tarp."

Fallon walked with Dan to the car and yanked back the canvas tarp. Underneath was a black, 2009 Porsche 911 Carrera Cabriolet.

"Whoa!" Dan said. "She's beautiful."

The car was in mint condition and just what Dan had spent the last three months looking for.

"She's a beaut," Mel agreed. "No Ferrari, but still pretty nice."

"Forty-five thousand?" Dan asked.

"Yep. Hate to see her go," Fallon said. "But Mother wants to move back to Oklahoma, and we're selling just about everything."

"Oh, yeah?" Mel asked. "What else ya got?"

Fallon tapped an index finger on his pursed lips. "Well, let's see. I got a fridge that's gotta go and a—"

"He's not buying anything, sir," Dan informed Fallon.

"I need a new fridge!" Mel pouted.

"You don't need a new fridge, the one in your room is fine."

"You selling a TV?" Mel asked.

"What the Christ? Maxine, can you take him back to the car, please?"

Mel turned and stomped off toward the car. "I'm gonna roll up the windows and sit in there like someone's old, neglected dog … and die from heat stroke!" he shouted as he climbed into the passenger seat and slammed the door.

Dan turned back to Fallon. "Sorry about that, Mitch. He's nuts."

"Dan!" Maxine scolded.

"Sorry. He's whatever politically correct name they have now for whack jobs."

Maxine shook her head.

Fallon said, "I understand. Got a brother-in-law that ain't got the sense God gave an oak tree."

Dan looked back at the car and rubbed his chin. "Would ya take forty?"

"How about forty-two?"

"You got yourself a deal, Mitch. What'll it take for you to hold 'er for me?"

"Five hundred should do it."

The two men shook hands. Dan pulled out his money clip and counted out a five Benjamins as a deposit. Together, Fallon and Dan tossed the tarp back over the car.

Dan thanked the man one last time and told him he would be back a little after five the next day with the rest of the money.

As Maxine pulled away from the house, Dan patted Mel on the shoulder. "Sorry I got after ya there, pal. I was trying to make a deal."

Mel shrugged. "It's fine."

"Don't be mad."

"You hurt my feelings."

Dan rolled his eyes. "What can I do to make it up to you?"

"Can we go to Red's and get a cheeseburger?"

"Sure, pal, and I could use a drink right about always."

Chapter Four

"Officer Mel Gormin!" Red called out from behind the bar, as Mel, Dan, and Maxine walked through the front door of Red's Bar and Grill.

Mel took a seat at the bar. "I told you, Red, I'm retired," he carped amiably. "I'm not a cop anymore. I'm a private investigator now."

Dan sat on his usual stool next to Mel, and Maxine headed straight for the restroom.

Red slid a glass of ice water across the bar to Mel. "Oh, that's right. Sorry about that, Mel. I'm just so used to calling you Officer Mel."

"Tequila, Seven, and lime," said Dan.

"Well, you're gonna have to get used to calling me just plain Mel, or Gormin, PI, if ya want."

Red filled an empty glass with ice. "Gormin, PI—that's catchy." He added a shot of tequila, a slice of lime, and filled the glass the rest of the way with 7Up. He set the drink in front of Dan.

"Say, Gormin, PI, why ya still wearing the badge, then?" Red asked.

Mel reached up and took hold of the aluminum foil-covered, cardboard badge that was hanging around his neck and looked it over. "It's a nice badge. My sister made it for me."

"How's your sister doing, Mel?" Red asked.

"Really good. Her and her boyfriend Steve are getting married this fall."

"Oh yeah? Hope we're all invited to the wedding."

"Of course you will be," Mel replied. "I'm going to be in the wedding."

"Best man?"

"No, just a regular old groomsman."

"Ever been in a wedding before?"

Mel eyes went downward and he stared through the bar top. "Just mine," he said quietly. "I liked the chicken dance."

Dan knew Mel was thinking about his wife who had been murdered years earlier. Dan knew the pain. Dan's own wife, Alex, had been killed in a car accident soon after the two had purchased the bungalow in Key West. They were only weeks away from moving to paradise; Dan moved down from New York alone—actually, not completely alone, his dog Buddy; who Dan blamed for the accident, came too—soon after Alex's funeral.

Dan reached over and placed his hand on Mel's back. "I'm sure they'll have a chicken dance at your sister's wedding," he said.

Red turned and grabbed a cup from the back bar and poured himself a cup of coffee. "So, what are you guys up to today?" he asked Dan.

"I have to run back out to Stock Island around five tomorrow and pick up my new car," Dan answered.

"You went with the Porsche?" Red asked.

"Yup."

"Nice," said Red with a grin and a nod.

"Not as nice as a Ferrari," argued Mel.

"What did ya give him for it?" Red asked.

"Forty-two grand," Dan replied.

Red whistled. "Must be nice, Mr. Got Rocks. Ever think of paying that Lotto jackpot you won forward—like, say, to little old me?" He batted his skimpy lashes.

Dan ignored him. "Probably gonna need a ride."

Red glanced back at the clock on the wall behind him. "Cindy comes in at four tomorrow, so I can give you a ride out then."

"We picked up a new case today too," Mel said excitedly. He had snapped out of his day dream down memory lane. "We're going to be bodyguards for a big movie star."

"Really?" Red asked.

"We don't know if she's a *big* movie star," Dan corrected. "We don't even know if she's a movie star at all. Her manager just said she was in the film industry."

"What else would she be?" Red asked. "Who else in the movie business would have a manager?"

"I don't know, maybe she's a writer, or a director or something."

"Do directors have managers?" Red inquired.

Dan shrugged his shoulders. "Who knows?"

Maxine walked out of the restroom and took a seat next to Dan.

"So, I hear Dan's gonna be protecting some young, good-lookin' starlet," Red jabbed.

"Yeah, I heard that too," Maxine said.

"Young? Good-looking?" Dan asked. "You people really know how to embellish a story."

"What can I get you, Maxine?" Red asked.

"I'll just have a cup of coffee, Red. Thanks."

Just then Jocko, the cook at Red's, walked through the stainless kitchen doors with a bucket of joint compound in one hand and a small putty knife in the other.

"Hey, Jock," Dan said.

"Yeah," Jock grumbled back.

"Whattaya doing there?"

Jocko turned and glared at Dan. "Fixing one of your messes again. What does it look like?"

"*My* mess?"

"Yeah, *your* mess. The goddamn bullet hole in the wall from yesterday. Remember that little fiasco?"

"Oh yeah. I can patch that if ya want me to."

Jocko continued over to the wall. "I wouldn't dream of it."

"And what do you mean, *again*?" Dan asked. "What other mess did you clean up?"

Red shook his head no and waived his arms trying to shut Dan up.

Jocko dropped the bucket and spun around. "Who do you think fixed that broken bar stool last week?"

"You," Dan responded.

"And who do you think fixed that ceiling fan the week before?"

"You."

"And who do you think removed the cowboy boot from the bathroom door and then hung a new bathroom door?"

"You. But in my defense, who wears pink cowboy boots? That guy had it coming."

Jocko's face was red. "It's not up to you to decide what color boots someone wears, or who has what coming, ya moron."

"I didn't tell him he shouldn't wear them. I merely pointed out that if he was *going* to wear them, then someone might make fun of him."

"Only an asshole like you, Coast. No one else gave a shit what color his boots were."

"Just because they remained silent doesn't mean they didn't hate the boots. I consider myself the voice of those who remain silent."

"Well I consider you the voice of every asshole in the world."

"Ouch!" said Dan. "That's a little hurtful."

Jocko just turned around and began removing the bucket's lid.

"Hey, Jocko, don't forget about the time Dan broke the front window!" Mel called out.

"Shut up, Mel," Dan said.

"Can I order my cheeseburger now?" Mel asked.

Red grabbed a guest check pad and said, "Order away, Mel."

Mel ordered a cheeseburger with fries, and Dan and Maxine both ordered a fish sandwich with fries.

Jocko dropped his putty knife into the bucket and went into the kitchen to fire up the grill.

When Red returned from the kitchen he poured himself another cup of coffee. "So are ya gonna need my help on this actress bodyguard thing?" he asked.

"Why would I need your help to babysit an actress?" Dan responded.

"There must be a reason her manager thinks she needs a bodyguard. What if someone attacks her—you gonna fight 'em off?"

"If I have to."

Maxine, Mel, Red, and Jocko all chuckled.

"I can fight!" Dan said angrily.

"Yeah, you can," Red agreed through his laughter. "Just like you did out in the parking lot a few months ago." Red turned to Maxine. "You should have seen him, Maxine, he looked just like Clubber Lang. First he hit the guy in the fist with his face, and then he hit him in the other fist with his ribs."

"The old one-two, I think they call that, Red," Mel offered.

Maxine turned and stared at Dan. "When did this happen?"

"Thanks, Red," said Dan. "Why can't you keep your big mouth shut?"

"Oh, sorry, I figured you told her about it," Red said.

"Oh, what a tangled web we weave," Mel added with a faux-cultured voice.

Dan slid his empty glass back across the bar. "No, I didn't tell her. Now, fill 'er up."

"So when was this?" Maxine asked again.

"The night the lawyer, Travis Holland, was killed," Dan informed her referring to the last case he had worked.

"Oh yeah," Maxine remembered. "The black eye you didn't want to explain."

"I didn't want to worry you," Dan said.

"Because what I don't know won't hurt me," said Maxine.

"Exactly," Dan replied.

Red pushed the refreshed tequila back in front of his friend.

The door opened and everyone turned to see who had come in; it was Ryan Jenkins. His arm was in a sling and he was wearing an ear-to-ear grin. By his side was a young black-haired woman; she was smiling as well. The girl was in her early twenties and at least fifteen years younger than Jenkins. Her skirt was short and her tight white T-shirt showed her belly. She wore too much makeup, but somehow it worked for her.

"Good afternoon, everyone," Jenkins said joyfully. "How is everyone today?"

"Wonderful!" said Dan. No one else answered.

Jenkins pulled an envelope from his back pocket and waived it in the air. "Got your money, Coast."

"Even more wonderful," Dan said.

Jenkins and his young friend walked up to the bar. "Princess, you sit right here," Jenkins said, pulling out one of the bar stools. Jenkins took her hand and helped her up onto the stool. "I would like everyone to meet Bunny McBride. Bunny, this is Dan Coast."

"Nice to meet you, Bunny," Dan said.

"And this is his friend Mel," Jenkins told her.

Mel jumped from his stool and walked over to Bunny. He took her hand in his and said, "Bewitching Bunny, it's a pleasure to meet you. You must be the whore who cuts Ryan's hair."

Chapter Five

It was four-thirty the next afternoon, Dan Coast sat on his front porch steps with a large manila envelope full of cash on his lap. Mel stood nearby in the front lawn fiddling with his homemade cardboard police badge dangling from a pink piece of yarn around his neck.

"Do you think I should keep wearing this badge even though I'm not a cop anymore?" he asked Dan. "You think it looks stupid?"

"Heavens no," Dan replied. "It looks completely normal for a grown man to wear an aluminum foil-covered cardboard badge hung around his neck by a pink piece of yarn."

"Yeah, that's what I thought. I just didn't want to look stupid."

"I don't think you have anything to worry about, Mel. This is Key West."

"Maybe I can have my sister make me a new one that says PI on it."

"PI?"

"For private investigator."

"Oh yeah."

Dan looked at his wrist to see what time it was, and then remembered there hadn't been a watch on his wrist since the day he moved to the Keys. He remembered it like it was yesterday. His realtor, Emily Dixon, handed him the keys to the bungalow at 632 Beach View Street. Emily hadn't smiled when she handed over the keys to the property, probably a first for her, Dan figured. Everybody knew his story; Key West was a small town, after all. Emily had kept her normally glib tongue in check and, like everybody else, pussyfooted around Dan and the aura of sadness that hovered around him like a foul stench. Dan grabbed the doormat from the front seat of his car, walked up the steps, and placed it on the porch floor in front of the front door. THE COASTS, stenciled in tasteful characters, stared up at him. Dan's late wife Alex had ordered the personalized doormat from a magazine a few weeks before they were supposed to make their move south from upstate New York. The mat arrived in the mail two days after her funeral. After staring at the mat for a few seconds Dan went to the bedroom, sat on the bed, and removed the watch his wife had given him as a gift. He opened the drawer to the nightstand, placed the watch inside, and shut the drawer. The watch had only left the drawer on a few occasions when Dan wanted to stagger down memory lane after a few too many tequilas.

"Dan … Dan," said Mel.

"Yeah, what?" Dan answered.

"Are you okay?"

"Yeah. Why?"

"You were just staring off like your mind was in some other place."

"Some other *time*, Mel," Dan whispered. "Some other time."

"When?"

"Red should be here any second," Dan said, changing the subject.

Mel turned to see the Firebird rounding the corner. "Here he is now."

Red skidded to a stop with the passenger side tires making a skid mark on Dan's lawn.

"Shotgun!" Mel yelled.

"Bullshit," Dan said as he opened the door and pulled the seat forward. "Get in the backseat, Mel."

"I get car sick," Mel argued.

"That might work with Maxine but it don't work with me. Now get in."

"Don't blame me if I puke on ya," Mel grumbled as he climbed into the back seat.

"Would you rather ride in the trunk?"

"No."

"Then shut up."

Dan pushed the seat back into place and climbed in.

"He's not gonna puke, is he?" Red asked.

"No," Dan answered. "That's just some bullshit he's come up with in the last few days."

"You're bullshit," said Mel defiantly.

"Ooh, good one." Dan glanced over his shoulder. Mel was shielding his face with his forearms, braced for the blow he was sure would come. "Like I'm gonna hit ya."

"You'd better not. I know karate." to demonstrate, he sliced the air with his flattened hands while making high-pitched battle cries that put Bruce Lee to shame.

Red pulled away from the curb. "Where to?"

"Head out to Stock Island and take a right on Cross Street." Dan reached down and fiddled with the radio until he got it tuned into 104.1; James Taylor was singing "Mexico."

When Red rounded the corner onto Twelfth Street, he quickly hit the brakes. Two patrol cars from the Monroe County Sheriff's Department and a van from the county coroner's office sat in front of Mitch Fallon's house.

"What the hell's going on here?" Dan asked.

Red slowed and pulled the car to the curb. "Is this the house?" he asked.

"Yeah, it is," Dan replied.

Mel gazed over the seat through the windshield. "I bet it's a homicide," he said.

"I'm sure it's not a homicide," said Dan.

"Should we get out?" Red asked.

"Yeah, I want to see what's going on."

"I bet Fallon killed his wife," Mel conjectured.

"Quiet, Mel." Dan opened his door.

"I'm just saying, he didn't seem like he wanted to move back to Oklahoma and he sure didn't want to sell that car." Mel climbed out and followed Dan toward the house. Red followed along as well.

One of the sheriff's deputies noticed the three men walking toward him and turned to intercept them. With his open hands chest-high he said, "This is a crime scene, guys. I'm gonna have to ask you to stay back a ways."

Dan looked around the property and then back at the deputy, whose nameplate read SIMMONS. "Did something happen to the Fallons?" he asked.

"Do you know the Fallons?" Simmons asked.

"I was out here yesterday morning." Dan pointed at the tarped Porsche. "I gave him a deposit for the car."

Simmons glanced back over his shoulder. "That car there?"

"Yeah."

"What time was that?"

"Ten-thirty … eleven, maybe."

"Did Fallon kill his wife?" Mel asked.

Dan said, "Shut up, Mel."

Simmons cocked his head at Mel.

"I'm a private detective," Mel informed him.

"He's not a private detective," Dan said.

"Am too," Mel argued.

Simmons pointed at Dan and Mel. "You two come with me." He stabbed a finger toward Red. "You wait out here."

Dan and Mel followed the deputy through the front door and into the living room.

"Jesus Christ," Dan whispered to himself when he saw the dead man seated in and tied to a chair in the middle of the room. A few feet from him, and lying on the floor, was another body covered by a white sheet.

A plain clothes investigator walked from the hall into the living room.

"Steve, this is Dan Coast," Simmons told the investigator. "He says he was here around eleven yesterday morning. He says he bought a car from the deceased."

"Special Investigator Steve Millhouse," he said, reaching out to shake Dan's hand.

Simmons turned and walked back outside.

Dan shook Millhouse's hand and then Mel shoved *his* hand at the investigator. "Mel Gormin, PI," he said.

"You're a private investigator?" Millhouse asked.

"Yes," Mel responded.

"No," said Dan. "He's not a private investigator."

Millhouse lowered his brow and looked to Simmons and then back to Dan. "Why did he say he was?"

Dan leaned into Millhouse and said conspiratorially, "Can we step over here for a second?" He and Millhouse walked a few feet away. Millhouse never took his eyes off of Mel. Dan leaned in and whispered, "He's a patient at the Lower Keys Psychiatric Center. He's staying with my girlfriend and me for the week; she's a nurse there. He used to think he was a cop, and now he thinks he's a private investigator."

Millhouse looked Mel up and down. "He's dressed just like Tom Selleck."

"Yeah," Dan explained. "That's his newest thing. It's best to just go along with it."

Millhouse agreed and together they walked back to the body.

"Is this the man you bought the car from?" Millhouse asked, pointing at the dead man in the chair. The man's head was back and his eyes were open. His hands were tied behind his back.

Dan shook his head. "No," he answered. "Mitch Fallon is taller, thinner, and a few years younger."

"This *is* Mitch Fallon," Millhouse said. "And that's Rebecca Fallon under the sheet. They put a bullet through her forehead right there on the floor."

"Christ," Dan said.

"When does the coroner put time of death?" Mel asked.

Millhouse was a little surprised by the question. "He's been dead at least thirty-six hours, and her ... around three hours."

"So you think Fallon was in here dead while I bought a car from his killer," Dan reasoned.

"Looks that way," Millhouse concurred. "How much did you give him?"

"It was a five hundred dollar deposit," said Dan. He gripped the envelope he was holding a little tighter.

"What's in the envelope, Mr. Coast?" Millhouse asked.

"Some money for the car."

"Over forty thousand dollars," Mel added.

"You have forty thousand dollars in that envelope?" Millhouse asked.

"He sure does," Mel replied. "He doesn't even work but he sure has a lot of money."

"Shut up, Mel," Dan ordered.

"Where did you get that kind of money, Coast?"

"My house," Dan answered.

"He keeps a bunch of money and a gun in a bag under his closet floor," Mel said.

Dan grinned nervously. "Quiet, Mel."

"Is there anything else in that bag under the floor that I should know about?" Millhouse asked.

"No," Dan replied.

"There's a cell phone and a couple pictures of girls," said Mel. "I think one of the girls is dead."

Dan put up his hand. "It's not like it sounds," he said.

"It never is, Coast," said Millhouse as he reached for the envelope. "I think I'm going to have you gentlemen come down to the station and answer a few more questions."

Dan dropped his head and handed the envelope to Millhouse. "What the Christ?"

Chapter Six

Red was waiting in the parking lot when Dan and Mel walked out of the Monroe County Sheriff's Department. Dan opened the passenger side door, pulled the seat forward, and Mel jumped into the back seat.

"Thanks for waiting," Dan said, climbing into the front seat.

"It's not the first time I've picked you up at the police station," Red reminded him.

"And it probably won't be the last," said Dan.

Red started the car and put it in drive. "Get everything squared away?" he asked.

"Yup. I had them give Rick a call. He explained everything."

"I bet he did."

Dan opened his envelope and began counting the bills. "Just want to make sure it's all here," he said. "It was out of my sight for about twenty minutes while they were on the phone with Rick."

"I doubt they stole any of your money."

"Ya never know." Dan pulled out his phone and began hitting buttons.

"Where to?" Red asked.

"Your place, I guess," Dan replied. "You getting hungry, Mel?"

"Yes, and I think I'm supposed to take my pills," Mel informed him.

"Swing by my house first, then. I'll grab his pills and then we can grab something to eat."

Red took a right off of College Road onto A1A.

"Goddammit!" Dan blurted out.

"What's the matter?" Red asked.

"Trying to access my email. I keep putting in the password but it says it's not correct."

"What's the password?" Red asked.

"I think it's buddythedog123."

"She changed it," Mel said.

"Changed what?"

"When you told that guy on the phone what your password was, Maxine changed it."

"What did she change it too?"

"I don't remember."

"Christ. Let me call her."

"Why do you need to check your email?" Red asked.

"That guy is supposed to send me information on the woman we're body-guarding."

"I don't think body-guarding is a word," Mel said.

"I don't think I give a shit," Dan replied as he punched in Maxine's number.

"Hello?" Maxine answered.

"What's my email password?" Dan asked.

"Maxinethegirlfriend123," Maxine replied.

"Oh, yeah, that's right. Thanks." Dan hung up.

"So what is it?" Red asked.

"She told me not to tell anyone."

Red rolled his eyes. "Don't you think we should all know it for the next time you forget it?"

"Good point," Dan agreed. "Maxinethegirlfriend123."

"Catchy," said Red.

"Kendra Hunt," Dan said.

"Who's Kendra Hunt?" Mel asked.

"She's the woman we're body-guarding. Ever hear of her?"

"Nope," Mel said.

"Sounds familiar," Red said.

"We'll have to look her up," Dan said.

"IMDb," said Mel.

"What's that?" Dan asked.

"Internet Movie Database, you moron," said Red. "Whenever there's a dispute in the bar about who played so-and-so in such-and-such a movie. IMDb clears it up pronto."

"I want to look her up, I want to look her up!" Mel begged. "Give me your phone, Dan."

"Okay, here." Dan handed his phone to Mel and Mel started tapping on the screen.

"It says here she's an actress," Mel retorted. "She's twenty-three years old, and she's from San Diego California. She's five-three, one hundred and ten pounds. She has blonde hair and she's *really* pretty."

"What's she been in?" Red asked.

"Let me see. It says here she's been in thirty-five movies."

"Wow," Dan said. "She must have started acting when she was a little kid."

"Nope," Mel said. "Says here she didn't start acting until she was eighteen."

"Thirty-five movies in five years?" Red asked.

"What are the movies?" Dan asked.

"Let's see," Mel said as he scrolled down her credits. "Big Wet Butts, Big Wet Butts 2, Big Wet Butts 3—"

Dan and Red quickly looked at each other. "That's enough, Mel, I think we got the idea," Dan said.

Mel continued. "Back Door Friends, Back Door Friends 2, Back Do—"

Dan spun around and snatched his phone away from Mel. "Give me that damn phone!"

"That's a lot of movies," Mel pointed out. "She must be really famous."

Red busted out laughing. "Yeah, I bet she is, Mel, I bet she is."

"Okay let's just drop it," Dan ordered.

Grinning, Red whipped out his iPhone and began pecking away.

"Now what are you doing?" Dan demanded, exasperated.

Searching Kendra Hunt on RedTube, waddaya think?"

"You're a pervert."

"Just being thorough. If we're going to protect this lovely lady, we need to … oh, my lord."

Mel craned his head forward and said, "I wanna see, I wanna see!" Red held up the iPhone for him. "Oh, my lord."

Dan asked, "What the Christ? Did you two just get religion?"

"Sort of," said Red, "Want to see living proof that there is a God, and he moves in mysterious ways?"

Mel darted his head this way and that, trying to see the action. "And so does Miss Hunt," he said wonderingly.

"God, you're both perverts! Put that thing away. You're corrupting Mel."

Red burst out laughing. "So, when's her plane arrive?" he asked.

"Day after tomorrow… at three in the afternoon."

"That gives you two days to break it to Maxine that you'll be body-guarding a twenty-three year old porn star."

"I was thinking I have two days to fake my own death."

Chapter Seven

It was a little after eleven thirty when Maxine walked in from work. Dan was in his recliner watching Perry Mason and working on his fourth tequila and 7Up.

"Hey," Dan said as she walked into the room and tossed her car keys onto the small table next to Buddy's bed.

"Hey," Maxine returned. "Where's Mel?"

"I killed him and buried him in the backyard."

Maxine walked over and gave Dan a peck on the cheek. "He get on your nerves today?"

"No, he was fine."

"Where is he?"

"Bed."

"Did you give him his medication?"

"Yut."

"All of it?"

"Yut."

"On time?"

"More or less."

"More, I hope." As she headed down the hallway she heard Dan turn up the television volume slightly. "Am I talking too much?"

"Yut."

When Maxine passed back through the living room on her way to the kitchen she was wearing a pair of black yoga pants and an olive-green Captain Tony's T-shirt. "I'm going to make a sandwich. You want something?"

"Sure."

"You want a sandwich?"

"No. just grab me that bag of Doritos."

When Maxine returned she was carrying a plate in one hand, a glass of milk in the other, and a bag of Cool Ranch Doritos between her teeth. She dropped the chips in Dan's lap.

Dan grabbed the chips and stood. "Here," he said. "Sit here."

"Thank you," Maxine said, and took a seat in the La-Z-Boy. She placed her glass of milk on the end table next to her. "You really need to buy another chair."

Dan grabbed a chair from the dining room table and slid it over next to Maxine. "I know, I know."

"I have tomorrow off. We should go to the furniture store and grab you a new chair, and maybe a couch." She took a bite of her sandwich.

"A couch *and* a chair? Who's gonna be sitting on all this furniture?"

"Whoever wants to."

"A couch and two chairs—that would be seating for like five or six people. When do I ever have that many people in my house?"

"I've seen that many people in your house before, a few times."

"Yeah, a few times, and on those rare occasions there's dining room chairs."

Maxine shook her head. "Like I said, I have tomorrow off, and we're going to the furniture store."

"You're not the boss of me," Dan mumbled.

"What was that?"

"Nothing."

"Did you have something to do tomorrow?"

"No, my new client doesn't get into town until the day after tomorrow." As soon as the words left his mouth, Dan knew there were questions coming his way, questions he did not feel like answering. He cleared his throat and suddenly felt a wave of guilt come over him. *Why?* he thought. *I haven't done anything wrong.* She's just a client, no different than any other client … except for the fact that she's a beautiful, twenty-three-year-old porn star.

"Oh, did that guy send you the information you were waiting for?"

"Yeah." He cleared his throat again.

"So, is she an actress?"

"Yes."

"Somebody famous?"

"Not real famous."

"What's her name?"

"Kendra Hunt, I think. I think that's what it was."

"Did he send you a picture of her?"

Dan felt as though he was sitting in a smoky room being interrogated by a homicide detective. The only thing missing was a spotlight in his face. "Yeah, he sent a picture."

"Is she pretty?"

Dan thought for a second. *How do I answer this? It's a no win situation.* "She's okay … I guess." His voice cracked. He felt his face redden and his mouth go dry.

Maxine caught it and shot him a look. "Just okay?" She furrowed her brows and gazed at him like a falcon staring down at a field mouse from thirty yards away. "What movies has she been in? Let me see the picture."

Dan was praying for a cerebral hemorrhage as he reached into his pocket for his cell phone. As he tapped the icons to open his email he was sure he had the same feeling in the pit of his stomach as a condemned man on his way to the electric chair. When the picture appeared on his screen he turned it toward Maxine.

"Oh, wow, she is pretty," Maxine said.

That was not the answer Dan was expecting. "I guess."

"You guess? She's gorgeous."

"She's not as pretty as you," slipped unconvincingly out of Dan's mouth.

Maxine laughed. "Yeah, right."

Dan stared at the television wondering how to derail the conversation.

"You can say she's pretty," Maxine informed him.

"Someone killed the guy I was buying the car from," Dan blurted out.

Maxine was sipping her milk and did a spit take. "What!" she hollered. "What do you mean, *someone killed him*?"

"Just what I said. Me, Red, and Mel went out to drop off the rest of the money and pick up the car, and when we got there a bunch of cops were there."

"Oh my God! Do they know who did it?"

Dan was grinning on the inside. *She completely forgot about the porn star. Thank God for murder.* "They think it was the guy I gave the money to."

"Wait a minute, I'm confused. I thought you gave the money to the guy who owned the car."

"No, evidently the guy I gave the money to was just pretending to be Mitch Fallon. The real Mr. and Mrs. Fallon were in the house dead when we were there."

"That's horrible."

"I know. I'll probably never see that five hundred dollars again."

"I mean those people being murdered was horrible," Maxine said.

"Oh, yeah, that too."

Maxine got up from the recliner and carried her empty plate and glass back to the kitchen. When she returned she said, "So, you never said—what movies has that actress been in?"

What the Christ! He took a deep breath and dove into the shallow end. "*Big Wet Butts* one through three and *Back Door Friends* one through seven, just to name a few."

Maxine was lowering herself into the La-Z-Boy and froze half way down. She raised an eyebrow and slowly turned her head toward Dan. "She's a porn star?"

"Adult film star," Dan corrected.

Maxine sat. "How do you feel about that?"

"Um, I feel exactly like you feel about it. How do you feel about it?"

"I feel fine about it."

"You do?"

"Yes. Why wouldn't I?"

"Because she's a porn star … and I'm a man."

Maxine laughed. "You're a man who's old enough to be her father."

"Well, yeah."

"If you were fifteen or twenty years younger I might be a little worried."

"Ouch."

"When she sleeps with men your age it's because someone is paying her to; it's her job. I'm sure she doesn't run around jumping into the sack with every forty-something-year-old man she meets."

Dan didn't know whether to be insulted or relieved. "Okay then, I guess we don't have a problem."

Maxine stood and held out her hand. "Come on, let's go make some porn of our own."

Dan took Maxine's hand. "I'm pretty old, but I'll give it the old college try."

"You didn't go to college."

As they walked down the hall toward the bedroom Dan said, "Well you've insulted my age and my education in the last few minutes. Anything you want to say about my penis before we get to the bed room?"

"Size don't matter?"

"Ouch."

Chapter Eight

The following afternoon—after hitting two furniture stores and not finding anything they could agree upon— Maxine dropped Dan and Mel off at Red's on her way to work. The two men sat on their usual stools drinking their usual drinks. Dan skimmed through the classifieds looking for a used mode of transportation. *One Particular Harbor* played on the old Wurlitzer.

Red stood behind the bar, one foot on the floor and the other on the bar sink. "So, what are ya gonna do about a car?" he asked.

"I don't know," Dan replied as he ran his finger down the page. "Keep looking I guess."

"What about that car you looked at over on Hutchinson Lane awhile back? Maybe that old guy hasn't sold it yet."

"I called, he did." Dan slid his glass across the bar and Red filled it up.

"You need another water, Mel?" Red asked.

Mel shook the ice in his glass. "No, thanks, I'm good."

Cindy walked through the door. "Gentlemen," she announced. Her boyfriend Derrick walked in behind her and took a seat next to Dan.

"What can I get you?" Red asked.

"Coke," Derrick answered. He turned to Dan. "You still looking for a car?"

"Yeah."

"Buddy of mine is moving up to Jacksonville. He's selling a 2014 Dodge Charger."

"Convertible?"

"No. Does it have to be?"

"It's what I was hoping for."

Red sat the Coke in front of Derrick. "Beggars can't be choosers," he said to Dan.

Mel pushed his glass to the edge of the bar. "I'll have a Coke, Red."

"No you won't," Dan said. "You know you're not supposed to have caffeine."

"I'll have another water then."

Derrick looked puzzled. "Who's your friend, Dan?" he asked.

Dan leaned back in his stool. "Oh, you've never met Mel?"

"I don't think so," Derrick responded.

"Derrick, this is Mel Gormin. Mel, Derrick White."

Mel laughed. "That's funny, because your name is White but yet you're black."

"Um, yeah," Derrick said.

Mel reached out to shake Derrick's hand. "It's nice to meet you. I'm a private investigator."

"Well that explains how you figured out I was black."

"I'm good at what I do." Mel sipped his water.

Derrick leaned in to Dan and whispered, "He's dressed like Magnum PI. Is he okay?"

Dan whispered back, "No, he's nuts."

"Oh."

Dan stabbed his finger into the paper. "Here's one. 2013 Jag Convertible, $52,600."

"I thought you were looking for a Porsche," Mel said.

"What's wrong with a Jag?" Dan pulled his cell phone from his pocket and dialed the number. "Hi, I'm calling about the Jaguar you have for sale."

"Yes, what would you like to know?" the person on the other end replied.

"You still have that?"

"We do."

"Can I swing by and take a look at it?"

"You can."

"Where are you located?"

"530 White Street."

"Twenty-five minutes good?"

"Sounds good."

Dan hung up the phone. "I need a ride."

Derrick and Red stared at each other, each waiting for the other to volunteer.

"Don't everyone speak up at once," said Dan.

"I'll give him a ride," Red finally said. He grabbed his car keys off of the back bar. "Come on."

"Let me finish this drink first," said Dan.

Cindy came back through the kitchen doors tying an apron around her waist and walked behind the bar.

Red removed *his* apron and tossed it under the bar. "I'll be back in a little while, Cindy. Ask Jock for the specials and put them on the board, will ya?"

Cindy began filling up the bar sink. "You got it."

Dan downed the last of his drink and he, Mel, and Red walked out the front door.

"Shotgun!" Mel hollered.

"Bullshit!" Dan hollered.

"I called it first," Mel argued.

"I don't care."

"He did call it first," Red said.

"Fine." Dan pulled open the door and climbed into the back seat.

Red drove out of the parking lot and headed up Seminole Street and took a left onto Reynolds Street. "Where's this place again?" he asked.

"530 White Street," Mel answered.

"Turn on the radio," Dan ordered.

Mel did as he was told and tuned it in to 98.7. Luke Bryan was singing "Crash My Party."

"This is country," Dan complained.

"*I* like country," Mel informed him.

"Since when?"

"Since I'm riding in the front seat and you're not."

"Ha!" Red said. "He got you there."

As they drove along White Street, Mel stared down each street they crossed. When they passed Duncan Street, Mel said matter-of-factly, "There's the same truck we saw yesterday."

"What truck?" Dan asked.

"The U-Haul," Mel answered.

"What U-Haul?"

"The one that was parked across from the dead guy's house."

Dan said, "Pull over, Red."

Red pulled to the curb and put the Firebird in park.

"Mel, are you telling me that you saw a U-Haul truck parked across the street from Fallon's house and now you just saw it again?"

"Yes, back there on Duncan Street."

"There's a lot of U-Haul trucks. How do you know it's the same one?"

Mel gave Dan a grin, shook his head, and in a condescending tone said, "Dan, Dan, Dan, I'm a private investigator. I'm a trained observer. I know it's the same truck because it has a big picture of a beautiful orange butterfly on the side, which means it's from Louisiana. You see, each state of origin has a different mural. For example, there's a submarine on the ones from South Carolina, and a giant squid on the ones from Newfoundland."

"What's on Nebraska?" Red asked.

"That's easy—ears of corn," Mel replied.

"Son of a bitch, he's right," said Red. "Saw one a couple weeks ago myself and admired the mural."

"Admired the mural?" Dan asked. "It was a decal on the side of a truck, not the Mona Lisa. Where was the truck parked, Mel?"

"In a driveway on the second block down, left hand side."

Dan pointed down the street. "Red, go down to Virginia Street and take a right."

Red put the car in drive and took the next right. He went up two blocks and tuned onto Florida Street and parked at the corner of Duncan.

"Open the door, Mel," said Dan.

Mel opened it and climbed out; Dan followed. The three men stood at the corner of Florida and Duncan and stared down the street at the U-Haul truck. Sure enough, a gulf fritillary butterfly mural decorated the broad side panel.

"Are you positive that's the truck?" Dan asked.

"I'm pretty sure," Mel said.

Red chuckled.

"Pretty sure?" Dan asked sternly.

"I'm almost positive."

"Almost positive."

"I'm 100 percent sure."

"Good enough."

"So, what's the plan?" Red asked.

Dan thought for a second. "How about if you walk down there and knock on the door."

"And then what?" Red asked.

"If someone answers the door," Dan instructed, "tell them you're there to look at the microwave they have advertised in the paper."

Red stared at his friend blankly.

"If it's the bad guys," Dan explained, "they'll show you the microwave. If it's the homeowner they won't know what the hell you're talking about."

"Sounds like a great plan," Red said sarcastically. "But I have one question."

"What's that?"

"What if they kill me?"

"What are the odds of that happening?"

"I don't know, I'm not a gambling man—but more than 1 percent is bad odds." Red turned back toward the U-Haul.

"Don't be such a baby, you've had a good life." Dan slapped Red on the ass. "Now get in the game, champ."

Red started walking down the street. "I gotta get some new friends," he mumbled.

"What's that?" Dan asked.

"Shut up."

Dan and Mel watched as Red neared the moving van. When he reached the front of the house he looked back, and Dan waved him on. Red shook his head and walked up onto the front porch of the light blue, single-story home and knocked on the door. He waited about twenty seconds and knocked again. He heard footsteps and then the door opened. A tall, thin, fifty-something-year-old man filled the door frame

"Can I help you?" he asked.

Red swallowed hard. "I'm here about the microwave oven," he said.

"Microwave oven?"

"The one in the paper. The one you have for sale."

"Oh, yeah, the microwave oven." The man pulled the door open farther and let go of the knob. The door hit the wall with a thud. "Come on in."

"Why?"

"So you can look at the microwave."

Red smiled nervously. "Right, so I can look at the microwave."

The man turned and headed toward the kitchen, Red followed.

Another man—a few years younger—stood in the living room. He was shorter, but more muscular. He wore red gym shorts and a tight blue wife-beater. On his feet were black Converse high-tops. He nodded as Red walked by; Red nodded back.

There were cardboard boxes on the kitchen counter and on the floor. Some of the boxes were filled with kitchenware. A coffee pot sat full on a Mr. Coffee machine and a plate of chocolate chip cookies sat on a plate next to the toaster.

"Here she is," the man said, waving his hand toward the microwave.

"Nice unit," said Red.

"I guess."

Red pushed some buttons and the oven turned on. "The carousel turns. Gotta light in there." Red hit stop and the interior went dark. "How much you say you want for it?"

"Fifty bucks."

"Hmm, fifty bucks," Red repeated. "How about forty?"

"You got yourself a deal, fella," he replied, reaching out and shaking Red's hand.

Red threw a thumb over his shoulder. "Those cookies fresh baked?"

When Red walked back around the corner onto Florida Street, Dan and Mel were leaning against the fender of his car.

"What the hell ya got there?" Dan asked.

"A forty-dollar microwave. What's it look like?"

"Wow!" Mel said. "She's a beaut, and only forty bucks, ya say?"

"Yeah," Red agreed. "She's a beaut all right, but I really didn't need another microwave."

"Then why did you buy it?" Dan asked.

"Because I was afraid they might kill me if I didn't."

"They?"

"Yeah, I saw two guys in there."

"Any sign of the homeowners?"

"No, but I only saw the living room and kitchen."

Dan's eyes went to his friend's chin. "What's that on your chin?"

"What?"

"Looks like chocolate," said Mel.

Dan looked closer. "It is chocolate."

"I had a cookie," Red said.

"A cookie."

"Two cookies."

"Did you bring us a cookie?" Mel asked.

Red glared at Mel. "You want a cookie, you march right down there and buy a refrigerator or something."

"I *need* a refrigerator," Mel responded.

"No you don't!" Dan exclaimed.

Chapter Nine

Mel and Red were sitting on the hood of Red's car and Dan was standing at the corner of Florida Street and Duncan Street keeping watch when Chief Rick Carver pulled up in his patrol car and parked behind the gold Firebird.

Rick hoisted himself up out of the driver's seat, adjusted his gun belt, pushed his gold-rimmed aviators back up the bridge of his nose, and looked around. "What do we got here, Coast?" he shouted to Dan.

Dan put a finger to his lips to shush Rick, and pointed down Duncan Street toward the U-Haul.

"This better be good," Rick said.

Red and Mel followed Rick to the corner.

"See that U-Haul parked in the driveway down there?" Dan asked.

"Yeah. What about it?" Rick responded.

"That's the same truck that was parked out front of the Fallon's house yesterday afternoon."

"The guy and his wife who were killed out on Stock Island?"

"Yeah."

"How do you know it's the same truck?"

"Well," Mel jumped in. "Each state has murals on—"

"It's got the same decals on the side," Dan said.

Rick looked from Dan to Mel and then back. "It's got the same decals because *you* say it does, or because"—Rick threw a thumb toward Mel—"*this* guy says it does?"

"Well, Mel noticed it was the same truck, but—"

"And you want me to walk down and knock on that door on the word of a mental patient."

"Hey!" Mel said. "That's offensive."

Rick ignored him.

"It's the same guy," Red offered.

"How the hell do you know that?" Rick asked.

"I saw him when I bought the microwave," Red replied. "He was just like Dan described him."

Rick looked confused. "You bought a micro—never mind. Alright, I'll walk down and take a look."

Rick started down the street and the other three followed close behind.

"Where are you Three Stooges going?" Rick asked.

"With you," said Dan.

"In case you need backup," Mel added.

"I don't need backup." He turned and started walking. His backup still followed, but hung farther back this time.

When he arrived at the rear of the moving van, Rick paused and peeked around the corner at the house. He glanced up at the huge butterfly decal and shook his head.

"What are you gonna do?" Red asked.

"I'm gonna knock on the door," Rick replied.

"Then what?" asked Dan.

"Just wait here," Rick ordered and walked cautiously up the steps to the front door. He knocked.

Mel turned to Dan and whispered, "You think there's any more of those chocolate chip cookies in there?"

"I hope so," Dan answered. "That's the only reason I called Rick and had him come down here, so you and I could get one of those cookies."

"Really?"

"No, not really. Now, keep quiet."

Rick raised his hand to knock again, but before his knuckles touched the wooden door, three shots rang out from inside the house. The first shot passed through the door and between Rick's left arm and his rib cage. The second clipped his ear as he stumbled backwards off the porch' and the third sailed over his head, ripping a king-sized hole in the neighbor's mailbox.

The three men hiding behind the U-Haul flinched in unison at the sound of the first shot.

Dan was on his way toward Rick as the third shot rang out. He grabbed Rick by his right arm and dragged him behind a traveler's palm.

Blood was flowing down the side of Rick's head and onto the shoulder of his shirt. He kicked at the ground with his heels as Dan dragged him along.

"The back door!" Mel shouted and bolted down the driveway.

"Mel!" Red yelled and went after him.

Rick grabbed the bloody mic clipped to his shirt and hollered for back up. "Officer down! Officer down!" he hollered into the mic. "Officer needs backup."

Dan yanked his shirt off over his head and pressed it against Rick's ear. "Keep pressure on this, Rick. I gotta go after Mel," he said, as he jumped to his feet and ran down the driveway.

Just as Dan entered the backyard he saw Red go over the fence. He leaped to the mid cross piece in the six-foot stockade, and with the palms of his hands on top of the slats, pushed himself up and over, landing in the backyard neighbor's lawn. Red and Mel were already out of sight.

When Dan got to Catherine Street he looked to his left—no one. He looked to his right to see Red rounding the corner onto Florida Street.

Dan was sprinting as fast as he could and knew he couldn't keep up the pace much longer; he was already having trouble catching his breath. Age, booze, and cigars were showing him who was in charge. Sweat ran in tiny streams from his pits and down his ribs. As he reached Florida Street he saw Mel entering Bay View Park. Sirens blasted in the distance.

Red had stopped between Eliza and Virginia streets. He was doubled over, his hands resting on his knees. Dan flew by him.

As Dan entered Bay View Park he slowed to a walk and looked around. Mel was nowhere in sight and neither were the two men he was chasing. "Son of a bitch!" Dan shouted, and then emptied the contents of his stomach onto the sidewalk.

*****

"I don't need to go to the hospital!" Rick shouted as the two paramedics struggled to raise the gurney and slide the large man into the back of the ambulance.

"You have to go," said Officer Terence Olivio. "That ear looks like hamburger meat."

Rick removed the bloody T-shirt from his ear and threw it at Dan, who was standing next to Olivio. "Here," he said. "Cover up those flabby tits, for Chrissakes. Nobody wants to see that."

Dan caught the shirt and glanced down at his chest with a shameful look. As they slammed the ambulance doors Dan mumbled, "He's one to talk."

Red sat on the steps, still trying to catch his breath; sweat dripped from his head and landed on the step between his feet.

The ambulance sped away and a Key West patrol car pulled up in its place; Mel was in the backseat.

"Ugh, thank God," Dan said.

The officer driving the unit got out and opened the back door to let Mel out. "Picked him up over on Palm Avenue," the officer said.

Mel climbed out of the backseat, a look of total devastation was plastered on his face. His shirt was torn and his Tigers ball cap was missing. "Sorry, Dan, I lost 'em." He hung his head down. "Lost my hat too."

Dan smiled. "Don't worry about it, pal, we'll get you another one."

Mel walked around the squad car toward Dan. "Probably better get a different one. I'm not good enough to wear a hat like Magnum."

Dan patted his friend on the back. "Sure you are, pal. Sure you are. You're one of the best private detectives I know."

"Thanks, Dan," Mel replied. "And you have the saggiest boobs of any private detective *I* know."

Chapter Ten

The alarm on Dan's cell phone sounded at six o'clock the next morning. He grabbed the infernal device from the nightstand and shut it off.

"What's going on?" Maxine asked, rubbing her eyes and rolling over.

Dan climbed out of bed and went to his dresser. "I was gonna go for a run before breakfast," he answered, pulling gym shorts from his dresser drawer.

"Wait … what? Running? Who are you and what did you do with my boyfriend?"

"Funny." Dan slipped on the shorts and an AC/DC T-shirt.

Maxine threw back the covers to reveal her very toned—and very naked body. "Want me to come with you?"

"No, that's alright. I was just gonna go a short distance. I won't be long."

"Are you sure? I'm a nurse. You might need someone to administer CPR."

"I used to run, ya know," Dan responded defensively.

"You were a lot younger then … and in a lot better shape."

"A *lot* better shape? Ouch."

He walked back to the bed and gave Maxine a kiss on the lips. He reluctantly pulled the covers back over her. "I'll be back shortly."

"Be careful. I love you."

"Back at ya," Dan replied, and went out the door.

Dan made his way through the living room past his dog, Buddy, who was lying on his puffy flannel bed next to the small table that held the framed photograph of his late wife, Alex. Dan glanced down at the photo on his way by. The hundreds of times they had run together along beaches, through cities, and on country roads flashed through his mind. His eyes shot to Buddy. The dog raised his head and their eyes met. Man and best friend had one thing in common: They shared one horrible moment in time, the loss of the most important person in the universe.

Dan stood with his back to the street with the toe of his sneaker on the bottom step. He pushed the heel of his foot toward the ground stretching his calf muscle, switched legs and repeated. He grabbed his ankle and pulled his foot to his butt cheek, then did the same with the other. He bent and tried to touch his toes; not gonna happen.

He ran across the yard, over the sidewalk, and into the street, waving to Edna MacGee, who was watching with great curiosity out her front window. Edna dropped the curtain when she saw Dan's wave.

It was seventy-five degrees and Dan was running into a light breeze. A seagull bounced across the street to claim

Dan grinned nervously. "It wasn't a shoot-out."

Mel turned and cocked his head. "What do you mean? Rick got shot right in the ear."

"*What?*" Maxine asked again.

"It's not as bad as it sounds," said Dan.

"I hope not, because it sounds really bad," Maxine said. "Was Rick shot, or not?"

Mel said, "Yes."

"It just grazed him," Dan replied.

"Oh, just *grazed* him," Maxine said sarcastically. "I guess that *is* nothing to worry about." She walked toward Mel. "Are you okay, Mel, honey?"

"I'm fine," Mel replied. "Don't worry about us. Me and Dan are probably the two best private investigators on this island."

"I'm sure you are, Mel, but you still have to be careful. Now, can you go out to the picnic table and I'll bring you your breakfast in a minute."

"Okay." Mel started for the back door, stopped when he got there, and turned around. "Are you going to yell at Dan?"

"No, Mel."

Mel walked outside and down the steps. Maxine pushed the back door closed and turned toward Dan. "You idiot!"

"Sorry."

"Sorry?" Maxine gasped. "He's our responsibility when he's staying with us. You have to stop doing things like this when he's with you."

"He's fine. Besides, I didn't know that was going to happen. We were on our way to look at a car."

Maxine walked back to the stove and flipped the French toast. "How did it turn from looking at a car into Rick getting shot in the head?"

"He didn't get shot in the head."

"The last I checked, the ear is part of the head."

"When we drove by Duncan Street, Mel recognized a moving van that was sitting in a driveway."

"Recognized it from where?"

"It was the same van that was parked in front of the house on Stock Island where we looked at the Porsche. Mel thought it might be a connection to the murders."

"Mel recognized the van? Mel thought there might be a connection? Well, I guess this was all Mel's fault."

Dan nodded his head. "Exactly. I promise from now on I'll keep a shorter leash on him so he won't get the rest of us in any trouble."

"You're an idiot."

Dan opened the back door. "I never said I wasn't." He picked his coffee cup up off the counter. "Can you bring my breakfast out too?"

"Where are you going?"

"Out to have a word with Mel. Don't you think he owes me an apology? He could have gotten me killed." Dan let the door slam behind him.

Mel was tossing a tennis ball out toward the beach when Dan walked up to the Adirondack chairs. Buddy glanced back at Dan and then took off after the ball.

"What time do we have to be to the airport?" Mel asked. He looked back over his shoulder to see Dan glaring at him. "What's the matter with you?"

"What do you think?" Dan answered.

"Um, you're mad at me?"

"Good guess."

"What did I do?"

Dan sat in one of the chairs. "Every time something happens you run in and tell Maxine."

"I walked in and told her."

"Same thing. You gotta learn when to keep your mouth shut. What happens when we're working a case is just between you and me. You don't have to tell her everything."

Buddy ran back to Mel and dropped the ball at his feet.

"Sorry," Mel said as he bent and picked up the ball. "I won't say anything from now on. I promise."

"Good."

The two men heard gravel crunching beneath someone's feet and turned to see Red coming down the pathway.

"Hey, Red!" Mel shouted. "You're just in time for breakfast."

"I was hopin'!" Red called back. He walked over and took a seat in the chair across from Dan. "So, what's the plan?" he asked.

"Hunt's plane arrives at 1:45," Dan said. "We'll head over to the airport around one."

"Sounds good," Red said.

"I wish we had a second car," said Dan.

"We can use my Ferrari," Mel suggested.

"Something that doesn't call a lot of attention to us," Dan said.

"I still have April's VW bug," Red offered. The car Red was referring to was a pink Volkswagen Beetle once owned by April Pantucco, wife of mobster Jimmy Pantucco. Red had purchased the car from Jimmy after April's death.

Dan nodded his head. "A pink Bug, just what I had in mind."

"Beggars can't be choosers," Red reminded him. "Besides, a little pink car is the perfect vehicle to use when picking up a young porn star."

"Adult film star," said Dan.

Chapter Eleven

Dan took a left off of South Roosevelt Boulevard onto Faraldo Circle and then into the parking lot of the Key West International Airport. He pulled the pink VW Bug into a parking spot and shut off the engine. Red and Mel, who were following close behind in Red's car, pulled into the parking space next to him. The three men climbed from the cars and walked across the parking lot toward the terminal.

Red checked his watch. "Her plane should be landing any minute," he announced to no one in particular.

The flight board said that American Airlines flight 4334 from Miami had arrived on time.

"Maybe this is them," said Mel, referring to a very over-weight couple in their fifties walking toward them.

"Does that woman *look* like an adult film star, Mel?" Dan asked.

"There is a thing called MILF porn, ya know," Mel shot back.

"I really don't think that woman falls into *that* category either."

Red chuckled. "I'm sure she falls into some porn category."

"None I want to watch," Dan assured him.

"You should have let me hold a sign with their names on it," said Mel.

"Shut up about the damn sign," Dan groused.

It was a little after two when Kendra Hunt and her manager Preston Harvey met Dan, Red, and Mel at the baggage carousel.

To Dan's eyes, Kendra was smaller in person than she looked in her photograph. Most celebrities were, in his limited experience, she stood about five-two and weighed maybe a hundred pounds. She was wearing baggy, dark brown sweatpants with SD PADRES written down one leg, and a white golf shirt, one size too big so as to hide what Dan presumed were bodacious physical assets, with all three buttons undone. On her head was a Padres baseball cap, and to finish the incognito look she wore Fendi cat-eye sunglasses that looked far too large for her small, freckled face.

He wasn't proud of it—but he wasn't ashamed, either—but as a card-carrying red-blooded male, Dan had sampled his share of porn in his younger days, more out of idle curiosity than prurient interest; when it came to sex, Dan liked to participate, not be a voyeur. From what he could see of her face, Kendra bore a passing resemblance to Bree Olsen, the girl next door-ish porn star Charlie Sheen had called his "goddess" during his well-publicized debauchery a few years back. She reminded Dan like any number of blond nymphets he had secretly ogled on the beach in his time—a wholesomely pretty girl who should be thinking about college or getting married, not banging strangers for a living.

Something about her brought out Dan's paternal instinct, too. He hoped she'd manage to escape from her sordid lifestyle and not become just another casualty of the chew 'em up, spit 'em out porn industry when her looks began to fade. Hell, she could be his daughter. Most assuredly she was somebody's daughter. All those lost girls were. Sleazebags totally devoid of morality preyed on their low self-esteem, promising glamour and wealth and fame. By the time they discovered the truth, it was too late to claw their way out of the abyss.

Sporting his gray Hawaiian shirt, white shorts, flip-flops, and Margaritaville ball cap, Preston Harvey looked like every other fifty-year-old man on vacation in the Keys. He did nothing to try to hide his middle-age paunch and had perfected a hairstyle that, like all comb overs, only drew attention to his baldness instead of hiding it. A ball of sleaze hung to him like a bad cologne, augmented by the chandelier of gaudy gold chains that dangled down into his forest of gray hair on his flabby chest.

"Harvey Preston?" Dan asked with his hand extended.

"Yes." Preston shook his hand. "You must be Dan Coast."

"I am." Dan motioned toward his two cohorts. "This is Red Baxter and Mel Gormin. They'll be working with me."

Preston stepped aside and introduced the young starlet. "This, gentlemen, is the beautiful Kendra Hunt, soon to be the most famous woman in adult films."

Dan nodded. "It's a pleasure to meet you Ms. Hunt."

Red reached out to shake her tiny hand. "Nice to meet you."

Kendra let it be known that she was not interested and turned toward the baggage carousel. She stared at the bags as they made their way around. "Why are my bags not here, Harvey?" she demanded impatiently.

"I'm sure they'll be out any second, Kendra," Preston replied. "Calm down."

Kendra's head snapped around so quick her pony tail smacked her in the face. "Don't you tell me to calm down. You drag me down to this god-forsaken island to dance at some shitty little bar. I'm nominated for three AVN Awards this year. I should be in Vegas, not here with these"—she waved her hand at the trio—"redneck … whatever they are."

Dan and Red looked at each other with eyebrows raised.

Mel stepped forward and held out his hand. "Miss. Hunt, it's an honor to meet such a beautiful young woman, especially one of such importance in the adult entertainment industry. On behalf of my colleagues, I would like to welcome you to our small slice of paradise."

"Well … thank you," Kendra responded. "That's very nice of you. Marvin, is it?"

"Mel, miss, Mel Gormin."

She took Mel's hand and gave it a slight shake. "It's very nice to meet you Mel Gormin."

When their hands released Dan stepped forward. "Miss Hunt, you will be riding to your hotel with me in one car, and Mr. Preston will be riding with Red and Mel in another car."

"I would like Mel to ride with me," said Kendra.

"Of course you would," Dan mumbled.

As Kendra walked past Red she looked up and said, "Be a dear and grab the bags, won't you?"

When they reached the parking lot Mel waved his arm at the pink Volkswagen Bug like Carol Merrill revealing what was behind door number two. "We secured a vehicle we felt would best represent your personality," he explained.

Kendra smiled as she walked around the vehicle. "I love it!"

"We knew you would," said Mel as he opened the passenger side door. "Would you like to ride up front, or in the back?"

"I'll ride in the back if you ride back there with me, Mel."

Mel pulled the seat forward and motioned for her to get in. "I sure will, Miss Hunt."

"Please, call me Kendra."

"My pleasure … captivating Kendra. I only hope I don't get carsick and barf all over you like a dog." Mel stuck his index finger in his mouth and pretend-retched convincingly.

To the surprise of all Kendra seized the same digit and plunged it into her own luscious mouth, sucking playfully for a long tantalizing moment while Mel's eyes bugged out of their sockets. Dan and Red were frozen in place.

Mel broke the silence with, "Ah, Kendra, how can you do that without gagging?"

Kendra tilted her cat-eye shades down to reveal her scintillating green eyes. "Practice, big boy. Now, get in!"

Red popped his trunk, placed the four suitcases inside, and slammed it shut. "What the hell is that all about?" he whispered to Dan.

Dan shrugged. "Who knows? Women seem to like him. He's got a certain disarming charm."

"I have to start acting crazier," Red said. "Maybe women will like *me* better."

"Yeah. Who knew bat shit crazy was the way to a beautiful woman's heart?"

Chapter Twelve

Dan Coast steered the VW around the circular driveway in front of the Atlantic Inn and stopped in front of the main entrance. Red pulled the Firebird in behind him. Two valets dressed identically in blue Hawaiian shirts and khaki shorts walked to the cars. Dan recognized one of the boys as Billy Denton, a longtime acquaintance he'd aided financially over the years

"Good afternoon, Mr. Coast," Billy said as Dan opened his door.

"How's everything going, Billy?" Dan asked.

"Good, sir."

Dan walked around to the passenger side of the car, opened the door, and pulled the seat forward. On the drive over, he'd glanced in his rearview mirror to make sure Kendra wasn't tutoring Mel in the art of porn acting and was relieved to see Mel had kept his fingers—and all his body parts— out of the starlet's mouth. As the smiling couple climbed from the vehicle, Dan surveyed the area, just like he had seen Kevin Costner do it in *The Bodyguard.*

Red had his trunk open and was grabbing the suitcases

The large glass double doors of the hotel slid open and out walked Michael Lord waving his hand above his head. "Daniel!" he called out. Michael was dressed just like the valets with the exception of a red shirt instead of blue. Unlike an old episode of Star Trek, a red shirt at the Atlantic Inn was a good thing.

Dan turned to see the young man walking toward him. "Michael, are the rooms ready?"

"Of course, Daniel. Two adjoining suites on the seventh floor, just like you asked. I had to move some people around and call in some favors, but anything for you sweetie." Michael winked.

"Thanks, Michael, I knew I could count on you."

Michael looked Dan up and down hungrily like a hyena in heat. "Oh, you can count on me for any of your needs, Daniel."

"Um, thanks?"

Michael led the group back through the doors, across the checkerboard floor in front of the registration desk, and to the elevators. "No need for a big star to register at the desk," Michael said over his shoulder. "We'll take care of all that later."

Kendra said nothing.

Red placed the luggage on a cart and motioned for a bell hop.

Michael, Dan, Kendra, and Mel all rode up in the first elevator. Red, Preston, and the luggage went up next.

Michael opened the door to room number 705. "Here's your room, Ms. Hunt."

Dan walked in first and Kendra followed. Mel remained in the hall.

Michael walked to 706 and unlocked the door. "Here you are Mr. Preston."

"Thank you," Preston said and entered his room, followed by Red and the baggage.

Michael unlocked the door that separated the two rooms. "Daniel, Mr. Preston's room has two bedrooms if you decide to stay here with them."

"Thank you, Michael," said Dan.

"If you need anything," Michael said, "please call the front desk and ask for me personally." He turned and swished back down the hall.

The bellhop waited at Preston's door. "That'll be all," Preston said.

The bellhop pursed his lips, turned, and walked out. Dan met him outside Kendra's door and slipped him a twenty. "Here ya go, Henry."

The boy smiled. "Thanks, Mr. Coast."

Dan stepped back into the suite and closed the door behind him. A hallway led from the door to a small living room, and a kitchenette beyond it. A bathroom was off the hall to the left and Preston's suite was through the open door on the right. The living room had a couch, two end tables with lamps, two matching chairs, and a desk. There were two bedrooms off of the living room, to the left, with an adjoining bath between them, accessible from each room. In the kitchenette was a little oak table with two oak chairs, a mini fridge, and a microwave. Beyond the kitchen was a sliding glass door that led to a balcony over-looking the pool. The roof-top pool sat level with the second floor. Preston's room was a mirror image of Kendra's.

Red had left Preston's suitcase on the floor in his suite, and then walked through the door with Kendra's luggage. "Where would you like these, Miss Hunt?" he asked.

Kendra sat on the edge of the sofa scrolling through her cell phone. "Right there is fine," she said, never looking up from the cell.

Red dropped the bags where he stood. They hit the floor with a thud, Kendra didn't notice.

Preston walked into the room. "How's your room?" he asked Kendra.

"I thought it would be bigger."

"This is one of the nicest hotels in town," Preston assured her.

Dan jumped in. "According to the itinerary you emailed me, Preston, you both will be staying in this evening."

That got Kendra's attention.

"Yes," Preston replied.

"No!" Kendra argued. "I will not sit in this room with nothing to do all night but stare at the TV. I wanna go out and do something."

"You're dancing at the club tomorrow night, Kendra," Preston reminded her. "Maybe you should stay in tonight and rest."

"Maybe you should stop treating me like a child, Harvey. I don't pay you to be my father, I pay you to do what you're told. I don't work for you; you work for me. Remember that."

Preston's face flushed and he looked around the room at the other men and then back at Kendra. "What would you like to do?" he asked.

Kendra laid her phone on the couch next to her. She looked up at Mel and smiled spontaneously; the big lug obviously brought out the best in her. "What would you suggest, Mel?"

Mel glanced over at Dan and then back at Kendra. "I don't really get out that much, Kendra. Dan or Red probably no more about the nightlife around here than I do."

Kendra looked at Dan. "What would you suggest, Dan?" She removed her ball cap and tossed it on the coffee table, then pulled the hair tie from around her ponytail and tossed it next to the cap. She scratched her head with her long red fingernails and her blonde hair fell down around her shoulders. "Where would a girl like me go to have a good time?" she asked with a seductive little grin. She leaned back on her elbow and crossed her legs.

The men who watched her movies would probably be impressed with the act but it was too late for Dan—he had already seen her for what she was: a spoiled little brat. "I have no idea, Miss Hunt. I don't know any girls like you," he answered.

The grin quickly left her face, and she sat up. It was obvious she hadn't been talked to in that tone of voice since her C-cups first made a showing. "What's that supposed to mean?" she shot back.

"Mr. Coast!" Preston admonished him.

"No, wait, Harvey," Kendra ordered, halting him with the palm of her hand. "Let him talk. What exactly do you mean, 'a girl like me'? What kind of girl am I?"

Dan folded his arms in front of him and cocked his head. "You're an immature and angry little girl who never grew up, and the reason you never grew up is because you thought *being* grown up had something to do with sex. You thought being mature meant being able to control people with sex and your looks, and now, with what little bit of money you've acquired through sex."

Kendra's face steadily grew redder as Dan kept speaking. When he had finished her teeth were clenched and she looked around for something to throw, finding only her phone. She grabbed it and hurled it at Dan's head while screaming, "Get out of my room! You're fired!"

The cell phone didn't even come close to its target, smashing instead against the wall to Dan's left and hitting the floor in three pieces. Dan glanced down at the floor and then at Preston. "Good luck," Dan said, and walked out.

Kendra looked at Mel. "Are you staying?" she asked.

Mel shook his head sorrowfully. "I'm sorry, but I have to go with Dan," he replied. Before he followed his friends out, he paused in the doorway to add guilelessly" "You know, Kendra, you really should work on your temper. It doesn't become a pretty young lady like you."

Kendra's mouth dropped open. "Mel, I'm sor—"

But he was already gone.

Chapter Thirteen

Dan and Mel sat on their bar stools at Red's Bar and Grill. "Love is My Religion" by Ziggy Marley played on the jukebox. Mel sipped his water.

There were three tables of four and two tables of two, all eating late lunches or early dinners. Cindy made her way around the room taking orders and delivering food. Jocko was behind the grill hollering, "Order up!" every so often and clearing tables when he had time.

"Well, that's gotta be a record," Red stated as he slid Dan's tequila, Seven, and lime across the bar. "Fired in less than two hours."

"I wasn't fired. I quit," said Dan.

"Her exact words were, 'Get out! You're fired!'" Mel reminded Dan.

"I said, 'I quit' before she ever said I was fired," Dan argued.

"I didn't hear that part," Red snorted.

"I said it to myself." Dan took a big gulp of his tequila.

"I don't think that counts," said Mel.

"It counts to me. Now, shut up and drink your water."

"So what are you gonna do now?" Red asked, as he poured himself a rum and Coke.

"Well, let's not forget there's still the tragedy from the other day to investigate."

Red nodded his head. "Oh, that's right, the double homicide."

"I was talking about the theft of my five hundred bucks, but solve one and you solve the other, I guess."

"Can I have five dollars for the jukebox?" Mel asked.

"No," Dan replied.

"I wanna play some songs."

"There's already songs playing."

"But I wanna play songs I like."

"Guitars and Tiki Bars" by Kenny Chesney was now playing.

"What's wrong with this song?" Dan asked.

"Nothing," Mel replied.

"Well, there ya go, a song you like. Just saved me five bucks."

"Dick," Mel muttered quietly.

Red busted out laughing.

Dan did a spit take. "Whoa! What?"

"I didn't say anything," Mel mumbled.

"I didn't think so," said Dan.

Still chuckling, Red turned to the open till of the cash register and pulled out a five dollar bill and tossed it in front of Mel. "Here ya go, pal. That was worth five bucks. He is a dick."

"Thanks, Red!" Mel said, jumped off the bar stool, and headed toward the old Wurlitzer

"Yeah, that's great," Dan said disgustedly. "Reward him for calling me a dick. Now he'll be doing it all the time."

"Why not?" Red guffawed. "Everyone else does."

Dan sipped his drink.

"Where should we start?" Red asked.

"Where should we start with what?"

"Getting back your precious five hundred dollars."

"I don't know."

"I wonder if Rick got anything on that U-Haul?"

"Let's start there." Dan pulled his cell phone from the pocket of his cargo shorts and dialed Rick's number.

"Hello?" Rick answered after a few rings.

"Hey, Rick."

"What do you want?"

"Geez, Rick, what makes you think I want something?"

"Because you only call when you want something."

"For your information. I was calling to see if you and Laura wanted to go to dinner tonight with me and Maxine. I was supposed to call you this morning but I forgot."

"Oh, okay. Let me call Laura and make sure nothing is going on. What time were you thinking?"

"We'll pick you up around seven."

"Sounds good, I'll get back to you quick as I can." Rick hung up his cell.

"You didn't ask about the U-Haul," Red pointed out.

"Well, no, I had to make up some bullshit story about going out to dinner so he wouldn't think I only called when I wanted something. I'll have to wait and ask tonight."

Red shook his head. "You're a real piece of work."

"I'll take that as a compliment."

Just as Mel returned to his seat at the bar "Happy Birthday" began playing over the speakers. Red and Dan looked at each other and then at Mel.

"'Happy Birthday'?" said Dan as if he'd been bitch-slapped. "*Really?*"

Mel shrugged. "It's one of my favorite songs."

"Is it someone's birthday?" Red asked.

"I'm sure it's *someone's* birthday," Mel replied. Mel turned to the patrons in the room. "Anyone celebrating a birthday today?"

A tall thin man in his early forties seated with his chubby, dark-haired wife and two small children put up his hand hesitantly and grinned. "Uh … I am," he responded.

"Hey!" Mel shouted excitingly. "Your meals are on the house! Congratulations!"

"Wow, thanks," the guy said.

"Everybody!" Mel hollered, raising his hands above his head. "Happy birthday to you. Happy birthday to you," he warbled in a pleasant enough baritone. When the entire room joined in, Mel's index finger became impromptu batons as he joyfully conducted the chorus.

Everyone was smiling and laughing … except Red, who now had to pay for four meals.

When the song was over everyone clapped and then returned to their meals.

"See why that's my favorite song?" Mel asked.

"Yeah," Red answered.

Dan snickered into his empty glass until his cell phone rang. "Hello?"

"It's Rick."

"I know."

"It's a go for dinner."

"Great. Pick you up at seven." Dan hung up the phone and slid his glass across the bar. He glanced over at Mel and then at Red. "How would *you* two like to spend some quality time together this evening?"

"Who two?" Red asked.

"You two," Dan repeated, waving his finger from Red to Mel.

Red said, "Um … I have—"

"That would be great!" Mel shouted. "We could go out and get something to eat, rent some movies. Oh, this is going to be great."

"Yeah, this is gonna be great," Red agreed half-heartedly.

"Can I spend the night?" Mel asked.

"No," Red quickly replied.

"Why not?" Mel asked.

"It's against my religion."

"Really? What religion are you?"

"Amish."

Mel cocked his head. "I did not know you were Amish, Red. See, we're learning new things about each other already. This is going to be great."

"Yeah, great," Red said. "Thanks, Dan."

"Don't mention it, my Amish friend."

Chapter Fourteen

At twenty minutes to seven Dan and Maxine dropped Mel off at Red's house on Rose Street. Mel carried a plastic Winn-Dixie grocery bag up the walkway toward the front door. Inside the bag were two DVDs—Dirty Harry and Magnum Force—and a checkerboard. Mel hoped the Amish played checkers. Mel also was anxious to ask Red why he didn't have a long funny beard.

Dan pulled away from the curb and sped off down the street the second Mel was inside and the door shut behind him.

Rick Carver and his wife Laura lived in a two-story home on Seventeenth Terrace. A wrought iron fence with cement columns surrounded the front yard. The stucco home was painted a light peach color with white trim and had a gray steel roof.

Dan steered Maxine's Blue Ford Focus to the curb and shut off the engine.

"Have you ever been out to dinner with Rick before?" Maxine asked.

Dan gave the horn a quick toot. "Never," he replied. "Breakfast and lunch a few times."

"Why dinner now?"

"Just trying to be nice. I feel a little like it was my fault he was shot in the ear." Dan craned his neck toward the front door to see if anyone was coming.

"I thought you were blaming that one on Mel."

"Well, yeah, it was Mel's fault, but I was supposed to be watching Mel. You know, the buck stops here, and all that shit. Besides, he helped me out quite a bit on the Victor Crawford case and I thought it would be nice to take him out to dinner for that too." Dan smacked the horn again, this time with the edge of his fist.

"Because you're such a nice guy," Maxine said suspiciously.

Dan ignored the jab. "Where are they," he whispered.

"Give them a second. We just pulled up."

Dan hit the horn again.

"Would you stop that!" said Maxine, slapping Dan's hand away from the steering column.

Dan opened his door. "Come on. Let's see what's taking them so long."

Maxine got out of the car and together they walked through the gate and to the front door.

Rick pulled open the door just as Dan lifted his fist to knock.

"In a hurry?" Rick asked. His entire left ear was wrapped in a bandage.

"I beeped three times," said Dan.

"In a matter of thirty seconds," Maxine added.

"How's the ear?" Dan asked.

Rick gently touched the bandage. "It wasn't as bad as it looked."

"Are ya gonna have half an ear?"

"No, they were able to stitch together both sides of what was missing. There'll be a scar, but it won't look too bad ... so they say."

Dan pretended to wipe sweat from his brow. "Thank God. I would have felt a little guilty if you had to join a circus as the one eared freak."

*****

Dan and Rick sat across from each other at the four top table at Louie's Backyard. Maxine sat to Dan's right, with Laura to Rick's right. Their table sat in the corner of the deck and over-looked the water. A dark blue umbrella, protruding through a hole in the middle of the table, was open but did nothing to block the setting sun.

Dan had a tequila, Seven, and lime in front of him, Rick was drinking a vodka and cranberry, and the ladies each had a bottle of Mic Ultra. They had ordered their meals and the menus had been removed from the table.

"So, Rick, you hear anything back on that U-Haul?" Dan asked. "With your good ear, I mean."

"As a matter of fact, I did, wise guy." Rick unfurled his napkin and placed it on his lap. "Is that why you asked me to dinner?" he added accusingly.

Dan hoped he didn't look guilty. "No, I was just trying to make conversation."

"Let's not talk shop," Laura pleaded. Her eyes went back to Maxine. "Maxine, I love that top you're wearing. The color goes great with your skin tone."

"Then let's not talk clothes either," said Dan.

Maxine smacked his arm. "Thank you, Laura. I bought this last summer and never wore it till now. The tag was still on it."

"The tags are still on half the clothes in her closet," Dan said.

Maxine shot him a look. "Really? At least I buy new clothes." She looked back at Laura. "Dan has underwear so old you can see through them."

"Most men do," Dan argued.

"I don't," said Rick.

Laura got up from the table. "Here, Rick, switch places with me."

Rick got up and did as he was asked.

Dan leaned in toward Rick. "So, what exactly did you hear about the U-Haul?"

"Why don't you just let the police and the sheriff's department handle this," Rick said.

"You guys can handle the murders, I just want my five hundred dollars back."

Rick rolled his eyes. "Two people were murdered and all you can think about is your money?"

"Yes."

"Fine," Rick sighed. "The U-Haul was rented on Big Pine Key."

"The renter have a name?" Dan asked.

"Probably, but he didn't give it."

"Did he rent it with cash?"

"Nope, Mitch Fallon's credit card. Even signed Fallon's name on the lease."

"Where did the coroner put Fallon's time of death?"

"*Mr.* Fallon had been dead about twenty-four hours, *Mrs.* Fallon only around three hours."

"Great dinner conversation," said Laura.

The two men ignored her. She shook her head disapprovingly and went back to her own conversation.

"I spoke to Fallon on the phone the day before, around noon," Dan said. "So they must have killed him shortly after."

Rick nodded his head yes. "Looks like. Then one of them drove to Big Pine, rented the van, and then returned to the Fallons' place"

"One of them stayed at the house with Mrs. Fallon. Any security cameras at the rental place?"

"Yeah, two of them. One outside with a view of the parking lot and one inside pointed at the counter."

"They get a picture of the guy?"

"No, he was wearing a hat and sunglasses. He kept his head down most of the time. He knew where the cameras were."

"So he had been there before."

"Probably. It wouldn't have mattered any way— footage from both cameras was pretty grainy. Probably couldn't have gotten a good picture of him even if he smiled and waved at the camera."

"How about the house on Duncan Street, learn anything there?"

"The Murphys. Coroner said they had both been dead less than two hours. We found them bound and gagged in a bedroom closet; both died from a gunshot wound to the back of the head."

"Talk to the neighbors?"

"We spoke to almost everyone who lives on Duncan Street. No one seemed to know the couple very well. Neighbors said they mostly kept to themselves."

"What's the next step in the investigation?" Dan asked.

"We're circulating the composite drawing based on the description you and Red gave to the sketch artist. Also, we're hoping one of them uses the credit card again—"

"Who ordered the salmon?" the waiter asked.

"Right here," Maxine responded.

He set her plate in front of her. "And the lamb chops?"

"That's me," said Laura.

"I'll be right back with the gentlemen's plates in just a second." He turned and walked back inside the kitchen.

Dan felt his cell phone vibrate in his pocket and reached for it.

Dan tapped the text message icon.

"Who's that?" Maxine inquired.

"Mel," Dan replied.

"What's he want?" Maxine cut into her salmon with the edge of her fork.

Dan read the text aloud. *How is dinner going?* He used his thumbs to text back *Fine,* and then put his cell away.

The waiter returned with Rick and Dan's steaks and placed their plates in front of them.

Dan's phone buzzed again. *Red won't play checkers with me.*

Dan texted back: *I don't care. Stop bothering me.*

Rick cut into his steak. "Perfect," he said, and took a bite.

Buzz! *You said to text you if I needed anything.*

I meant something important. Don't text me unless ur on fire.

Dan cut into his steak. Buzz! "What the Christ!" Dan read the message. *What if Red is on fire?*

Dan didn't respond to the text this time and shoved the phone back in his pocket.

"Maybe you shouldn't have bought him that cell phone," Maxine said.

"Ya think?" Dan took another bite of his steak and washed it down with the last gulp of his tequila. "Where the hell's that waiter?" Dan's phone vibrated again; he ignored it.

"So, who exactly is this Mel?" Laura asked.

"He's a friend of Dan's," Maxine replied with a smirk.

"A friend of mine?" Dan shot back.

"He stays with us every once in a while," Maxine explained.

"And where do you know him from, Dan?" Laura asked.

Rick smiled. "Yeah, Dan, tell Laura where you know Mel from."

Maxine answered for him. "Dan and Mel met during Dan's court-appointed stay at the Lower Keys Psychiatric Center."

Dan glared at Maxine and then looked around the deck. "Where the Christ is the waiter? I feel like I'm in rehab here." He took a sip of the melted ice. His phone buzzed again and he clenched his jaw.

"Oh, yeah," Laura said. "At Christmas time last year. I had forgotten about that. How are you feeling now, Dan?"

"I'm feeling fine, Laura. I was feeling fine then. I didn't go because I was crazy. I went because the judge said I had to."

Rick laid his hand alongside his mouth and cocked his head toward his wife. "That's what they all say."

Maxine and Laura laughed out loud.

"Oh. My. God. That is so hilarious, Rick," said Dan. "You are one funny guy." His phone went off again, it was ringing this time. "Christ!" He started to reach for the phone but noticed the waiter out of the corner of his eye. He went for his glass, raised it over his head, and shook the ice frantically.

The waiter gave him a dirty look as he walked over. "Can I get you another drink, sir?"

"Yes, please," Dan answered.

The waiter turned with a thinly disguised scowl and headed toward the bar.

Dan cut into his steak and stabbed the chunk with his fork.

"Excuse me," a female voice said.

Dan looked up from his meal to see the forty-something hostess hovering above him, an apologetic smile on her face.

"Excuse me," she said again. "Are you Dan Coast?"

"Yes."

"There's a call for you at the bar. The gentleman said it's urgent."

Dan grabbed the cloth napkin that lay over his lap and tossed it on the table. "Thanks," he said. He looked to the group. "I'll be right back."

When Dan got to the bar he said to the bartender, "I'm Dan Coast, there's a call for me."

The bartender pointed at a phone that sat at the end of the bar. The receiver lay on its side next to the phone.

Dan walked over. "Hello?"

"Dan?" Mel said.

"Yeah. What's the matter?"

"Red wants to watch Magnum Force *before* Dirty Harry."

"Holy fuck! Ya gotta be shittin' me," Dan said sarcastically.

"No, I'm not."

"I didn't think anyone was that stupid."

"I didn't either."

"You tell him that I said if he doesn't watch Dirty Harry first I'll come back there and shove both those movies up his ass."

Mel snickered. "Thanks, Dan."

"No problem, pal. Now, please don't call or text me again tonight."

"Okay."

"We'll pick you up in a couple hours."

"Okay. Red! Dan said you have to watch Dirty Harry first."

"Hang up the phone, Mel," Dan said.

"He said he's going to shove both movies up your butt."

"Mel, hang up the phone!"

"You better do what he says!" Mel hollered.

"Or what?" Red shouted back.

"Hang up the—Christ." Dan hung up the phone and returned to the table.

"Everything okay?" Maxine asked.

"Compared to what?" Dan asked.

Chapter Fifteen

At ten-thirty the next morning Red walked through Dan's front door. He was carrying a Styrofoam cup half-full of coffee. "Am I too late for breakfast?" he asked.

Maxine sat at the dining room table sipping coffee and flipping gingerly through the Key West Citizen. "Dishes are done and the kitchen is closed," she informed him.

"Damn!"

Mel sat in Dan's La-Z-Boy in front of the television watching a moldy rerun of Rosanne. "I could make you something," he said. "But they won't let me use the stove."

Red feigned surprise. "The bastards."

"You're lucky we let you use the microwave," Dan said as he walked into the dining room from the kitchen.

Red took a sip of his coffee through the torn plastic lid. "So, what did you learn from Rick last night?" he asked.

"Not much," Dan answered. "Someone kept calling and texting me all night."

Mel's index finger shot into the air. "That was me!"

Dan made his way over to the giant dry-erase board on wheels he kept against the wall. "I think this looks like a good time to use the *case board*."

Red crinkled up his nose. "Still going with the name case board, huh?"

"Until someone comes up with something better."

Dan grabbed the two sketch artists' renditions he had lying on the table. One was of the man he had given his five hundred dollar deposit to, and the other was the second man Red had seen, and described to the police, at the house on Duncan Street. He inserted each drawing into its own magnetic clip and stuck it to the case board. Then, he wrote DAN'S MISSING MONEY in red marker.

"Dan's missing money," Red read aloud. "So, we're gonna just forget about the four people who were murdered."

"For now," said Dan.

Red rolled his eyes.

In blue marker Dan wrote UNSUB under each drawing.

"Unsub?" Red asked. "What's unsub?"

"Learned that on Criminal Minds. Means unknown subject."

"I learned that at the police academy," said Mel.

"Shouldn't it be hyphenated?" asked Red.

Dan stepped back and gazed at the word. "What are you, a goddamn English teacher? It's fine the way it is."

"I think it *is* hyphenated," Mel agreed.

"*I* would think so," said Red.

Dan turned to the two men. "Is *shut the hell up* hyphenated?"

"I'm not sure," Mel answered.

Maxine stared at the newspaper with a big smile on her face.

"Okay," Dan began. "Rick said the coroner placed Mrs. Fallon's time of death—"

"TOD!" Mel shouted.

"—at around 2:00 PM. Mr. Fallon's TOD—"

"Thank you," said Mel.

"—was around twenty-four hours earlier." Dan drew a horizontal line across the entire board making a time line as he spoke. "After they killed Fallon, one of the men—the taller of the two—went to Big Pine and rented the U-Haul van with Fallon's credit card. The other one stayed at the house with Mrs. Fallon. I answered the classified ad Monday after breakfast and then we drove out there a little while after."

"Fallon was already dead at this time," said Red.

"I'm figuring he was still alive when I phoned, but dead by the time we arrived. I gave the five hundred dollar deposit to one of the killers—"

"Poor, poor, Dan," Red said.

"Anyway, after giving him the deposit we left and didn't return to the Fallon house until around five the next day."

"And," Red added. "they figure these two guys kept Mrs. Fallon alive until around 2:00 pm."

"Correct." Dan backed away from the case board and rested his chin between his thumb and index finger.

"So what does this tell us?" Red asked.

"Absolutely nothing," Dan responded.

Mel muted the television. "How are we going to catch these guys?" he asked.

"I have no idea," said Dan.

"Maybe they were targeted because they were moving," Maxine said.

Everyone looked at Maxine.

"What?" Dan asked.

"Maybe the victims were chosen because they were moving," Maxine repeated.

"No one said they were moving," Dan informed her.

"Mr. Fallon told us they were moving back to Oklahoma."

"But that wasn't really Mr. Fallon."

"No, but maybe Fallon told the killers they were moving and that's why the *unsub* told us."

"Doesn't sound very likely," Dan argued. "The cops questioned the neighbors. Rick didn't say anyone told them they were moving."

Maxine counterpunched with: "He also said none of the neighbors knew the Murphys very well, so maybe no one knew they were moving."

"There was no 'for sale' sign in front of the house," Red said.

"There was no 'for sale' sign in front of the Fallon's house either," Maxine argued.

"You got a point there, Maxine," said Mel.

Maxine smiled. "Thanks, Mel."

"No she doesn't have a point," Dan said. "We don't know that anyone was moving anywhere, and even if the Fallon's were moving, it doesn't mean anything."

"No, but maybe this does," Maxine said, her index finger pointing at an item in the newspaper. "Look at this story on the last page of the state news."

Dan walked up behind her and looked over her shoulder. The headline at the bottom of the page read ALLENTOWN COUPLE FOUND MURDERED IN THEIR HOME. He leaned in for a closer look as Maxine summarized the article.

"It says here the couple had been missing for three weeks. Their house had been sold and everything had been moved out. Neighbors said they remember seeing a U-Haul truck out front, and two movers loading their stuff into it. When their son, who lives out of state, hadn't heard from them in a couple of weeks, he phoned the police. The couple was discovered shot dead in their old home."

"Does she have a point now?" Red asked.

"Shut up, Red," Dan shot back.

Maxine continued. "I say we search online for couples who have been murdered right before they were supposed to move."

"Okay," Dan said. "You do that."

"But I have to go to work," Maxine reminded him.

"You sit at a desk in front of a computer most of your shift. You can do a couple searches."

"Are you saying I'm not busy at work?"

Dan cocked his head and stared at her.

"Okay fine, I'll search it." She got up from the table and headed down the hall toward the bedroom.

Red stared at the case board. "So, what's next?"

Dan thought for a second. "Maybe we should run a classified ad—moving sale."

"Who's moving?" Mel asked.

Dan turned to Red.

Red put up his hands. "Not me. They know what I look like."

"Can't be me either," Dan agreed. "They've seen me … and Mel, and Maxine."

"How about Skip?" Maxine called out from the bedroom.

"We'll get Skip to do it," said Dan.

"Good idea, Dan," Mel said.

"It was my idea!" Maxine shouted.

"Ignore her," said Dan. He wrote the words MOVING SALE in the upper right hand corner of the dry-erase board. "How should we word it?"

"Everything must go!" Mel shouted, startling Dan.

"Okay." Dan jotted down *everything must go*.

"Put an exclamation point at the end," Mel directed.

Dan did as he was asked.

"The best part about this plan," Red said. "is now I can sell that damn microwave I bought."

"You should probably give the microwave back to the Murphys," said Dan, as he stared at the case board.

"They give me forty bucks and they can have it back."

"The Murphys are dead, but I'll give you forty dollars for the microwave," Mel said.

"Sold!" Red shouted.

"No, Mel" Dan said. "You're not buying the microwave."

"But I need a microwave."

"What the Christ! Why did you have to bring the damn microwave up again?" Dan jotted down Skip's cell phone number under the words everything must go.

"Shouldn't we ask Skip first?" Red suggested.

"No," Dan replied. "The longer we keep him out of the loop, the less time we'll have to deal with him. Come on, let's head over to the newspaper office first."

Mel jumped out of the recliner. "Shotgun!"

"Shotgun's ass," Dan said. "You're riding in the back."

"I get carsick."

"No ya don't. Let's go."

Red headed out the front door, followed by Dan and Mel. Dan was almost to the door when he heard Maxine shout, "Bye!"

"Oops." Dan spun on the balls of his feet and hurried to the bedroom. "Bye," he said, and pecked Maxine on the lips.

"Love ya," she said.

"Back at ya," he said.

Mel was already sitting in the front seat with the door shut, and his seat belt buckled.

"In the back," said Dan.

Mel unbuckled his belt, climbed over the center console and into the back seat. He sat with his arms folded, staring straight ahead. "Dick," he mumbled.

"What's that?" Dan asked.

"Nothing."

Red put the old Firebird in drive and headed off down the street.

They hadn't made it three blocks from the house when Dan and Red heard *Hurk! Hurk!* From the back seat. They ignored the first two. But on the third Hurk! Dan spun his head around.

"What the Christ are ya doin'?" Dan asked.

Mel was halfway through an over-animated convulsion. "Eerff! I'm gagging. I think I'm getting carsick."

"You're gonna be *my-boot-up-your-ass* sick in about two seconds, if ya don't knock it off," said Dan.

"You better not puke in my car," Red warned him.

Mel let out one more *Hurk!* and rolled his shoulders forward, then he was done. He slumped back in the seat defeated.

Chapter Sixteen

It was 3:00 am when Dan Coast heard his cell phone vibrate across the top of his nightstand. He rolled over and fought to open his eyes. The display light lit the entire room. He thought he was dreaming, until Maxine jabbed him in the back with her elbow.

"Are you going to get that?" Maxine asked. Her voice was grumbly. She cleared her throat in a most unladylike fashion.

"What?" Dan asked.

"The phone."

The cell vibrated again.

"Yeah," Dan said, and reached for his phone.

"Who is it?" Maxine asked him.

"Hold on. What?"

"Coast?" said a man's voice. "It's Preston."

"Who?"

"Preston Harvey."

"What do you want?"

"It's Kendra, she's disappeared."

"Disappeared? Where did she go?"

"If I knew that, I wouldn't be calling you."

"It's two in the morning."

"*Three* in the morning," Maxine corrected.

"*Three* in the morning," said Dan.

"Coast, ya gotta help me," Harvey pleaded. There was much concern in his shaky voice. "I can't find her anywhere. She won't answer her cell phone and she's not responding to my texts."

"Try checking the last place you saw her. That always works for my car keys. If she doesn't turn up, call the cops."

"I already phoned the pol—"

Dan ended the call. He rolled back and pressed his body against the warmth of Maxine's back. He put his arm around her and ground his pelvis into her butt cheeks.

"Problem?" Maxine asked.

"Yeah," Dan replied. "You're wearing underwear."

"I mean with the phone call."

"Preston Harvey is missing his porn star."

"Adult film star," said Maxine.

Dan pressed hard against her.

"I have to get up in two hours."

"I'm up now," Dan whispered. He put his hands on her back and began to massage her shoulders, slowly working down to the small of her back.

Maxine snored.

Dammit! Denied. Dan pulled back the covers, slipped on his boxer shorts that were lying on the floor, and went to take a leak.

On his way back to the bedroom, Dan paused at Mel's door, it was open just a crack. He pushed it open a few inches farther and peeked into the room. It was dark and he waited for his eyes to adjust. When they did, he could see the bed was empty. He reached in, flipped on the ceiling light, and entered the room.

Where the hell is he? Dan wondered. He turned and walked down the hall toward the dining room. "Mel," he whispered loudly, and waited for an answer. There wasn't one.

Dan turned on the dining room light. Buddy was lying on his flannel bed. He lifted his head and looked at Dan.

"You seen Mel?" Dan asked.

Buddy didn't say a word.

Dan went into the kitchen and turned on the light, he even went to the back door and looked out into the yard. When he returned to the dining room he saw the note on the dining room table.

Dan,

Kendra called my cell phone.

She said she needed my help.

Didn't want to wake you. Call you later.

Your best friend,

Mel

P.S. Don't blame Buddy. I asked him not to say anything.

"Sonofabitch!" Dan grabbed the note and brought it back to the bedroom with him. "Hey," he whispered. Then a little louder: "Hey!"

Maxine stirred. "We'll do it tomorrow night, I promise. I have to get up early."

"Maxine," Dan said. "Mel's gone."

She shot up in bed. "What! What do you mean, gone?" She threw back the covers and hurried to Mel's room. "He's gone," she said.

"I know. That's what I'm saying, he's gone. I checked the whole house."

"Where did he go?"

Dan handed Maxine the note. "Sonofabitch!" she said.

"That's what I said."

Dan and Maxine's eyes shot to the small table that sat next to Buddy's bed, the table where the picture of Alex sat, the table where Maxine dropped her car keys whenever she got to Dan's. The keys were gone.

"Sonofabitch!" they said in unison.

Chapter Seventeen

Preston Harvey was waiting out front of the Atlantic Inn Hotel when Dan and Red pulled up in Red's car. Dan hopped out and pulled the seat forward. "Get in," he said.

Harvey climbed into the back seat. "Where are we going?"

"To find Mel," Red said.

"What about Kendra?" Harvey asked.

"If she's with him, we'll find her too."

Dan dialed his cell phone for the sixth time since discovering Mel had left the house.

Hello, the voice mail message said. You've reached the Gormin Detective Agency, Mel Gormin PI speaking. I can't take your call right now, probably because I'm out solving crimes at the moment, because I'm a private investigator, just like Magnum, PI. I also have a Ferrari like Magnum, PI. Wait … what was I saying? Oh yeah, I can't come to the phone right now but if you leave a mess—" The message cut off.

"Mel, it's Dan again. Call me back if you get this message." Dan hung up his cell and turned to Harvey. "Where did you see Kendra last?"

"She danced and signed autographs at a place called Secret Treasures, on Duvall Street tonight," Harvey said. "You know of it?"

"No," said Dan.

"Yes," said Red.

Red took a left off of Caroline Street onto Duvall and parked across the street from the Secret Treasures Gentlemen's Club.

"Come here often?" Dan asked as he climbed from the car.

"Once," Red responded. "For a stag party."

The three men crossed the street. A towering bear of a man in faded jeans, and a red flannel shirt with the sleeves cut off was closing the front door of Secret Treasures. The black bouncer pulled a set of keys from his front pocket and inserted one into the lock.

"Excuse me," Dan said.

The man turned. "Sorry, guys, we're closed."

"We're looking for a girl," Harvey said.

The big guy chuckled, flashing an amiable grin that spotlighted a single diamond on his left incisor. "That's why they come here."

Harvey said, "We're looking for Kendra Hunt."

"She took off about two hours—hey wait, aren't you the guy that was with her?"

"Yes," Harvey replied. "I'm her manager. I haven't heard from her since she left here and I'm trying to get in touch with her."

The big lug laughed again. Everything seemed to be funny to him. When he wasn't laughing, he was smiling. "I'm sure she's being taken care of quite well."

"What do ya mean?" Red asked.

The big man turned toward Red. "Oh, hey, Red, didn't notice you."

"Hey, Carl," Red responded. "You know where Kendra went?"

Dan looked from Red to Carl. "Yeah, Carl, do ya?"

"She left with Hammer Jones. That's where I'm headed now. He's having a party over to his place on Cindy Avenue. Y'all can follow me over if ya like."

"Who the Christ is Hammer Jones?" Dan asked.

Carl snickered. "Good one. Like you don't know who Hammer Jones is."

Carl's car was parked right in front of the club. "Right this way, gentlemen," he said, and climbed into his black 2012 Audi.

Dan and his group ran across the street and jumped back into Red's car. Red made a U-turn and then followed Carl onto Eaton Street.

"Two things," Dan said. "First, who the hell is Hammer Jones?"

"Running back for the Gators from '02 to '05. How could you not know that?"

"Okay. Second, how come I've never met your friend Carl before?"

"He's not my friend, he just works at the club," Red said defensively.

"He knew you by your first name."

"He probably knows a lot of guys by their first names." Red veered right onto Palm Avenue.

"Yeah," Dan agreed. "Guys who hang out at the strip club."

"It's a gentlemen's club," Red corrected him.

"Then how did you get in?"

Harvey leaned forward and stuck his head between the two men. "Anyone ever tell you two guys you bicker at each other like an old married couple?"

Dan stared straight ahead. "Anyone ever push you out of a moving vehicle?"

"Ha!" Red snorted as he took a left onto North Roosevelt Boulevard.

Harvey quietly slumped back into his seat.

When Red rounded the corner onto Cindy Avenue, Dan immediately noticed Maxine's blue Focus parked at the curb, on the left side of the street, facing the wrong direction. Several other cars were parked on the street as well.

Dan pointed at the Focus and Red nodded. Red pulled to the curb directly across from Maxine's car. Carl pulled into the driveway.

Dan climbed from the car and looked over the roof of the Firebird toward Hammer Jones's house. Mel was in the front yard climbing to his feet and brushing grass clippings from his knees. Two large men were walking away from Mel on their way back to the house. Dan and Red ran to Mel's side.

"You okay, Mel?" Dan asked.

"Where's Kendra?" Harvey asked when he reached the three men.

Mel pointed toward the house. "She's inside. I'm sorry, I tried to get her out of there but two guys dragged me out here."

"It's not your fault, pal," Red reassured him.

Dan looked back at the house. The thumping bass from the music could be heard throughout the neighborhood. Every light in the place was on and the blinds and curtains were open.

"How many people are in there?" Dan asked as he stared through the windows.

"Maybe thirty," Mel answered.

"His parties are usually pretty rowdy," Carl added.

"Good thing we brought our own bouncer with us," said Red.

Carl looked around, and then grinned. "Oh, you mean me."

"Yeah, you," Red replied. "I'm hoping we can count on you."

"I'm here for ya, Red," Carl said.

"Aw, that's beautiful," said Dan. "Now, let's go get 'er."

"I'll wait out here," Harvey said.

Red reached out and grabbed Harvey by the back of the shirt. "No ya won't."

Dan entered the front door first, followed by Mel. Red brought up the rear, pulling Harvey along with him. Carl almost had to turn sideways to fit his shoulders through the thirty-six inch wide opening. Hip-hop was blasting from an unseen stereo; the jacked up bass was turning Dan's bones to jelly. He looked around the living room, which contained mostly men, and then he heard cheering coming from another room. He made his way toward the excitement.

A few of the guys, mostly in their late twenties and early thirties, glanced over at the group as they moved through the house, but didn't seem too concerned and went back to high-fiving, calling each other bro, and telling whatever lies it was they were telling.

In the middle of what most people would use as their dining room, Dan spotted Kendra standing on top of a pool table. She was dressed only in a white lace G-string. A crowd of men, three and four deep, stood around the pool table hollering and clapping. Some were shouting for her to dance, others kept yelling, "Take it off!"

Kendra's small hands were covering her breasts and tears were streaming down her cheeks as she halfheartedly gyrated to the music.

"Dance, ya whore!" one guy with a shaved head shouted, then he threw an empty beer can at her, she ducked and the can flew past her head.

When she came back up she spotted Dan, and a look of relief spread across her face.

Dan pushed his way through the crowd until two men shaped like semi-trucks separated him from Kendra. He reached up and grabbed one by the shoulder and tried to move him out of the way. The guy didn't budge.

Red pushed Dan aside and grabbed the behemoth by the arm and spun him around.

"What do ya think yer doin', Pop?" the guy asked.

Red hit him in the ribs with a right and landed a left jab on his nose

Dan tried to squeeze through.

Another bruiser grabbed Dan by the shoulder. "Hold on," he said, and yanked Dan backwards. Dan slid backwards on his ass across the floor. The bruiser's attention went back to the table-top show.

Dan jumped to his feet and kicked him in the crotch as hard as he could from behind. The bruiser grabbed his balls, dropped to his knees, and slammed his chin on the edge of the pool table.

"Hold on's ass," said Dan.

The guy Red hit stumbled backwards a few steps and then came back at Red. Carl stepped in and connected with a haymaker to the puss that sent the man sailing like a paper airplane across the pool table, where he landed unconscious at Kendra's feet.

Carl turned toward the crowd. "Anybody else?" he shouted. The crowd backed away.

Dan grabbed Kendra by the wrist and pulled her over his left shoulder.

Someone tried to grab Kendra's ankle. Mel hit the man in the throat with the back of his hand and then gave him an elbow to the jaw. The man stumbled back against the wall holding his throat and gasping for air.

"Anybody else?" Mel hollered.

Carl exploded in throaty laughter. "Nice, Mel!" he shouted above the music.

Dan headed for the exit with Kendra over his shoulder. Just before he reached the open door a hulk of a man stepped in front of him. A white tank top was tucked into his shorts. The talons of the bald eagle on his shirt gripped a banner that read AMERICAN AS FUCK.

"Where ya going with the entertainment?" Hammer Jones asked politely. He skimmed a dinner plate-sized hand over his spiked hair that made him look vaguely like the GoDaddy dude.

"Out of here," Dan answered.

"I don't think so," said Jones. "I paid a lot of money for that little bitch." He grinned, and when he cracked his knuckles every vein in his body bulged.

"Aargh!" Dan heard behind him, and stepped aside just as Carl charged past him hitting Jones just below the rib cage with his shoulder. Jones's feet left the floor and the two men were halfway across the front yard before they hit the ground with a thud.

The two men wrestled for a second, then they separated, both getting to their feet.

Jones swung a right at Carl's head. Carl dodged the meaty fist and brought up his own hands.

Jones swung again.

Carl ducked and came back up with a hard right under Jones's chin, stunning the big man.

Jones took two steps back and came at Carl again.

Carl swung with a right. Jones blocked it.

Carl threw a left. Jones blocked it.

Jones slammed his forehead into Carl's nose. Carl stepped back, wiped the blood from his upper lip, and looked at it.

"That's gonna cost ya," Carl said. He ran at Jones tackling him again.

Jones was on his back with Carl on top of him. Before Jones could even get his hands up, Carl had hit him in the face five or six times—first a right, then a left, over and over again.

When Jones's arms dropped to the grass Carl stopped. He wiped his nose again and got to his feet.

Dan was already putting Kendra into Maxine's car.

Red hurried to his own car with Harvey close behind.

As Mel walked by Jones he gave him a swift kick to the ribs. Jones made an *Umph* sound as some air escaped his lungs.

"Later, bro," Mel said, and ran to join Red and Harvey.

As Carl was climbing back into his Audi he shouted over the roof: "Catch ya later at the club, Red!"

With Dan glowering at him, Red gave Carl a sheepish wave.

Chapter Eighteen

Red led the way down Flagler Avenue back toward the Atlantic Inn; Dan was close behind.

Dan looked down at the clock in the dashboard. 4:45. *Maxine is probably up now and getting ready for work*, he thought. He reached into his pocket for his cell phone, and then, for the first time since getting into the car, he looked over at Kendra.

Kendra sat with her legs pulled up under her as though she was trying to make herself as small as possible. She was still wearing nothing but her underwear. Her right forearm did its best to cover her breasts. She had stopped crying but dark mascara trails were dried upon her cheeks. She stared out the window at the early morning sky.

Dan glanced behind him. A white sweater of Maxine's lay in the backseat. He reached back, grabbed it, and tossed it to Kendra. She pulled it over her shoulders.

"Doesn't seem worth the money," Dan said.

Kendra ignored him.

"How much do you make for something like that?" Dan pressed.

Kendra continued to stare out the window. "Something like what?"

"Dancing naked on a pool table in front of a bunch of drunken assholes while they throw empty beer cans at you and call you names."

Kendra didn't answer.

"Where are your parents?" Dan asked.

She gave Dan a snotty look. "I'm an adult," she snapped back.

"*I'm* adult, too," Dan said. "and I *still* have parents."

"Well, so do I. Big deal."

"And I asked where they are."

"None of your business."

"I think what happened tonight kinda makes it my business."

"Oh, why, because you think you rescued me? You're a real hero."

"*Think* I rescued you?"

"I can take care of myself."

"It didn't look like it."

"You think you're so smart."

"Smart enough not to dance on a pool table naked for a has been college football player who still wears denim shorts and tucks in his tank top like it's 1992."

Kendra smiled. "You left out his spiked hair."

"He could poke an eye out with that head."

Kendra laughed. She was silent for a moment and then said, "Nothing."

"What?" Dan asked.

"You asked how much I made. I didn't make anything."

"Then why did you go?"

"Jones seemed nice at the club. He said he was having an afterhours party at his place and wanted to know if I wanted to go with him. I thought it might be fun."

"You didn't know you were the entertainment."

"No."

"Jones said he paid good money for you."

"I don't know what he meant by that."

Dan rounded the corner onto Duvall Street.

"Where are you taking me?" Kendra asked.

"Back to the Atlantic Inn."

Kendra sighed. "Isn't there somewhere else we could go? I'm really hungry. Can we get something to eat?"

"You're naked."

Kendra looked down and pulled the sweater tighter. "Oh, yeah."

Dan whipped a U-turn. "We'll go to my place."

*****

Dan pulled Maxine's car into the driveway of his modest beach bungalow at 632 Beach View Street and shut off the engine. The sun hadn't come up yet but the sky was slowly turning from black to purple to blue. The porch light was on as well as the living room light.

When Dan climbed from the Ford Focus he glanced across the street at Mrs. MacGee's house. As usual she was standing at her front window like a sentry on duty. She let the curtain drop back into place when she saw Dan look.

She don't miss a thing, Dan thought.

Kendra got out of the car and looked around. "This your place?" she asked.

"Yep. Home sweet home," Dan replied.

They walked up the steps onto the porch and Dan opened the front door. As Kendra stepped up to the doormat she looked down and read THE COASTS.

"You married?" she asked.

"No." Dan stepped aside and motioned for Kendra to enter. He closed the door behind them.

Maxine, dressed in her dark blue scrubs and white Crocs, exited the kitchen holding a hot cup of coffee. She stopped dead in her tracks.

"Good morning," Dan said.

"Good morning," Maxine responded.

"Good morning," Kendra said.

"Good morning," said Maxine.

"I'm Kendra."

"I'm Maxine."

"And I'm Dan," Dan said, clapping his hands together.

"Where's Mel?" Maxine asked.

"He's fine. He's with Red," Dan replied.

Kendra walked toward Maxine with her hand extended. "It's nice to meet you, Maxine."

Maxine took her hand and gave it a slight shake. "It's nice to meet you as well, Kendra. Can I get you something … coffee … clothing?"

Kendra smiled foolishly. "Both would be nice."

"Dan, make Kendra a cup of coffee" Maxine said, and then started down the hallway. "I'll grab her something to put on."

Dan headed for the kitchen.

When Maxine returned to the living room she was carrying a gray, long-sleeved T-shirt of Dan's that said Salt Life on the back and again down one of the sleeves, and a pair of her own black stretch pants. "Here you go," she said, handing the clothes to the young woman.

"Thank you," said Kendra. She removed the sweater she was wearing. Maxine glanced down at the perfectly sculpted breasts and quickly turned her head. "Let me see what's taking him so long."

Dan was pouring coffee into a mug when Maxine walked into the kitchen.

"How do you think she likes her coffee?" Dan asked.

"I have no idea," Maxine replied. "Why don't you ask her?"

"How do you like your coffee?" Dan shouted.

"Black!" Kendra hollered back.

Dan picked up the mug and turned. "Are you okay?" he asked.

"Why wouldn't I be?" Maxine inquired.

"Because I brought her here."

"I'm sure men bring home naked porn stars to their girlfriends in the wee hours of the morning all the time."

Dan grinned. "Only in heaven."

"Funny."

"Hey, I thought you said you weren't worried about Kendra because I'm an out-of-shape old fart."

"I wasn't, until I saw her perfect boobs."

"They're perfect? I want to see!"

"You'd better not."

Kendra was sitting in the recliner flipping through the TV stations when the two walked back into the living room. Dan handed her the coffee.

"Thank you," Kendra said.

"Would you like something to eat?" Maxine asked.

"I don't want to put you to any trouble."

"It's no trouble," Maxine assured her.

"I'm sorry about this," Kendra said.

Dan heard a noise at the back door and went to investigate.

"Sorry about what?" Maxine asked.

"Having him bring me here. I'm sure I'm not the type of person you want in your home."

"I don't know what type of person you are."

"You know what I do for a living."

"Yes."

"Does it bother you?"

"I'm not going to judge you because of what you do for a living, if that's what you're asking."

Kendra's eyes went to the television for a second and then back to Maxine.

Maxine pulled a chair from the dining room table and sat down so she could see the television as well.

Kendra looked her up and down. "You must be a nurse."

"Bingo." Maxine sipped her coffee.

"I wanted to be a nurse when I was a little girl. Obviously *that* didn't happen. But I've played a nurse in a few of my movies. Probably not the same thing, though."

Maxine thought back to Dan's stay at the Lower Keys Psychiatric Center and their first sexual encounter in the janitor's closet. "You might be surprised," she said.

Kendra cocked her head but didn't pry.

Dan walked into the room with his dog, Buddy, close behind.

"Our guest would like something for breakfast," Maxine informed him.

"Um, okay." Dan spun on his toes and returned to the kitchen.

Kendra watched as Buddy lumbered over to his bed and laid down. "He's very well behaved," she commented.

"He's getting better," Maxine said as she watched her boyfriend leave the room. "He's cut down on his drinking quite a bit and he's following simple commands now."

Kendra looked at Maxine and then toward the kitchen. Both women burst into laughter.

"What's so funny?" Dan called out.

"Nothing!" Maxine shouted back.

Chapter Nineteen

After Maxine had gone to work and Kendra had eaten her two eggs, bacon, and toast, she fell asleep in the recliner; Dan tossed a thin blanket over her and quietly went out the front door.

Dan sat down on the top front step. Today's Citizen lay neatly folded next to him. He glanced at the weather forecast—perfect, like most days in paradise—while reaching into his pocket for his cell phone. Seven missed calls. *Shit*. He dialed.

"Hey, it's me," said Dan. He picked up his cup of coffee from the step and took a drink.

"Where the hell have you been?" Red asked angrily.

"We're at my house."

"I figured. You might have had the courtesy to let me know, asshole. I almost came looking for you two. Why didn't you take her back to the hotel?"

"She didn't want to go."

"So you brought her to your house."

"Yes."

"What did Maxine have to say about that?"

"Nothing."

"Nothing?"

"Nothing."

"Huh. Hold on a sec." Dan heard Red's muffled voice reporting: "Everything's cool. They're at Dan's house."

"You still with Harvey?" Dan asked.

"Yeah. He was getting pretty worried."

"I bet he was. Wouldn't want anything to happen to his cash cow."

"What do you mean?" Red asked.

"Hammer Jones made a comment that he paid a lot of money for Kendra to entertain his guests."

"And?"

"And Kendra said she wasn't paid, that she just went there because Jones invited her."

"You think Harvey set it up?"

"That's what I'm thinking. Probably why he called me instead of the cops."

"Probably."

"How's Mel doing?" Dan asked.

"He's sound asleep."

"Can you wake him up and get him over here? He needs to take his medication before the satellites start following him and the chem-trails start infecting him."

"Sure thing," Red said. "We'll be there toot sweet."

"The tooter the sweeter," Dan replied, and then hung up. The door opened behind him and Kendra walked out onto the porch holding a mug of coffee. Dan scooted over and Kendra sat down beside him. "Beautiful day," she commented.

Dan idly scanned the headlines in the Citizen. Damn, she smells good. "They all are," he said.

"The beach is right behind your house?" she asked.

"Yep. I got a package deal. The beach came with the ocean."

Kendra managed a delicate little smile. "I live on the beach too, in Malibu."

"Oh, yeah?"

"Have you ever been?"

"To Malibu?"

"Yes."

"No."

"It's beautiful. Maxine went to work?"

"Yes."

"Most women wouldn't go to work and leave their boyfriends home alone with a porn star."

"Most women aren't Maxine."

"And I would imagine most boyfriends aren't you."

Dan smiled. "I guess."

"Thank you … for last night."

"It was just eggs and bacon."

"You know what I mean."

"Don't worry about it. All in a day's work."

"But I fired you."

"What about Harvey?"

"What about him?"

"You threatened to fire him at the hotel the other day."

Kendra blew into her mug and then sipped her coffee. "Yeah, but I would never do it. Everything I am, everything I have, I owe to him."

Dan stared at the young girl but remained silent.

"What?" Kendra asked.

"Nothing," Dan responded.

"If you have something to say, say it."

Dan took a breath and slowly exhaled. "You said everything you are and everything you have you owe to Harvey."

"Yes."

"What do you have?"

"What do you mean?"

"You said you live in Malibu, on the beach."

"Yes."

"Do you own the house?"

"No. The production company owns it."

"What do you drive?"

"A 'vette."

"Is it yours?"

"It belongs to Preston."

"Who pays you?" Dan asked.

"Preston pays me."

"If he works for you, then why aren't you paying him? Does he work on commission?"

"He gets 10 percent plus."

"Plus? What's the plus?"

"I don't know. He just says 10 percent plus. I guess the plus is for the things he has to pay for for me."

"Like clothes?"

"I guess."

"And the beach house, and the Corvette?"

"Sure, I guess." Kendra took another gulp of her coffee.

"So the house and car are his and you're paying for them."

Kendra thought for a second. "You're confusing me," she said.

"Do you have a lawyer?"

"Preston has a lawyer. *He* handles everything. Can we talk about something else? I'm not good with money and stuff."

"Sure, we can talk about something else."

Kendra sat with her elbows on her knees and her chin resting on the rim of her coffee mug as she held it with both hands. She stared off across the street. "Why does that old lady keep staring out her window at us?" she asked.

"That's Mrs. MacGee, Beach View Streets very own neighborhood watch program."

"I feel safe."

Dan stood. "Come on. Would you like to meet her?"

"Meet her? Why?"

"If I know Edna MacGee, she has probably just taken fresh-baked muffins or something out of the oven and she has a fresh pot of coffee on."

Kendra got to her feet. "I guess."

As they walked across the street Dan said, "Besides, it'll be fun to watch the look on her face when she finds out you're a porn star."

Chapter Twenty

When Dan and Kendra returned from Mrs. MacGee's, Red, Mel, and Preston Harvey were seated around Dan's dining room table. Red had fixed them all breakfast and made a fresh pot of coffee.

"You're out of eggs," Red informed Dan.

"And bread," Mel added.

"I'll put those items on the list," Dan said sarcastically.

"Where were *you* two?" Harvey asked.

"Across the street," Dan replied. "Talking to a neighbor."

"Old Lady MacGee?" Red asked.

"Yes," said Kendra. "Very nice lady."

Harvey shoved a piece of toast into his mouth before he spoke. "What did she think of you?" Harvey asked.

"She said I was a delightful young lady."

"Didn't tell her what ya did for a livin', did ya?"

"As a matter of fact, I did."

Harvey gave a sleazoid chuckle. "The old bag clutch her chest?"

"Worse," Dan replied. "She proceeded to tell us about the art film she appeared in while she was in college back in the fifties. Full frontal nudity, as she described it."

"Eesh," spluttered Red.

"She's a beautiful woman," Mel offered. "I can just picture her naked now."

"Please don't," said Red. "The image might be contagious."

Harvey mopped up the last of his egg yolk with his remaining toast and shoved it into his pie hole. "Who's giving us a ride back to the hotel?" he asked, getting up from his chair.

"Red," Dan said. "Can you give them a ride back? I'm gonna take Mel with me over to Skip's. The ad came out in the paper this morning, and he'll probably be wondering why he's getting a bunch of phone calls."

"Sure thing," said Red.

*****

Skip Stoner lived at the corner of Flagler Avenue and Seventeenth Street in a small block house painted a funky green, about two blocks down from the Quik Mart where her worked. It was a modest one-story home with two bedrooms—but way out of the price range of a man who worked part time at a gas station, but then again, a lot of things about Skip never seemed to add up.

Skip's house had no driveway. A concrete apron ran from the street to the sidewalk, but a driveway had never been installed, probably for fear of losing most of the back yard. Dan parked the pink Volkswagen Bug on Seventeenth Street behind Skip's bright yellow 1974 Volkswagen Thing.

"Can I ring the doorbell?" Mel asked, as they walked across the street.

"I don't give a shit," Dan replied.

They stepped upon to Skip's covered concrete patio and Dan quickly rang the bell.

"Hey!" shouted Mel

"What?"

"You said I could ring the bell."

"Oooo, I forgot," said Dan. "Go ahead and ring it if you want."

"Too late now."

"Ring it … ring it."

As Mel reached for the button, Dan slapped his hand away.

"What did you do that for?" Mel asked.

"I think I heard him coming," Dan replied.

"I didn't hear anything."

"Oh, probably because I forgot to give you your ear pills this morning."

"I take ear pills now?"

"Yeah. Didn't Maxine tell you?"

"No."

"Maybe I didn't hear anything after all." Dan rang the bell again.

"Hey!"

"What."

"I could have rang it that time."

"Go ahead," Dan said.

Mel raised his hand and the door opened. "Dang it!"

Skip had his cell phone to his ear and raised his wait-a-minute finger. "I have no idea what you're talking about, dude," he said in his Jeff Spicoliesque manner. "I'm not moving anywhere." He took the phone away from his ear and hit the end call icon. "People are so rude these days." He pushed open the screen door. "Dan the Man and his sidekick, the Melinator! Come on in, dudes."

Dan walked in, followed by Mel. They sat at Skip's kitchen table.

"Can I offer you boys a cup of coffee?" Skip asked. "It's instant, but it does what it's supposed to—give you a buzz or make you take a shit. Or if ya want I can whip up a fresh pot."

"No, thanks," said Dan.

"Yes, please," Mel replied.

"He doesn't want any coffee," Dan said.

"I'll have a water," said Mel.

"So, to what do I owe this awesome pleasure?" Skip asked as he made his way to the cupboard for a glass.

"We put an ad in the paper," Dan explained. "It says you're having a moving sale."

Skip sat the glass of water in front of Mel. "Well that explains the three calls I've had this morning. Why would you do that? Are ya tryin' to get rid of the old Skipster?" There was a note of genuine hurt in his voice.

"No, nothing like that, Skip," Dan reassured him, although the thought had occurred to him many times before. "Here's the deal: We're trying to catch two guys who stole five hundred bucks from me. We think they're targeting people who are getting ready to move."

"It was Maxine's idea," Mel said.

"It was not," Dan argued.

"Yeah. Remember she said—"

"Quiet, Mel."

"So, you're working on a case," Skip said, "and you need the old Skipster's help."

"No," Dan replied. "We just need to use your house. These guys have already seen Me, Mel, and Red."

"Oh," said Skip. "So what's the plan, Dan the Man?"

"Just keep your cell phone on you and when people call about your moving sale, give them your address and tell them they can come by and look at the stuff any time tomorrow."

"Why tomorrow? Why not today?"

"Because the day is almost half over and Red is busy today. Tomorrow will give us time to get things set up here."

"Set up? What do you mean, set up?"

"We'll put some price tags on things, make it look like it's a real moving sale. Make things look legit."

"What if the guys who took your money show up?" Skip asked.

"Red, Mel, and I will be hiding in the other room. We'll set up my camera and stream it live. We'll be able to see what's going on in here on our cell phones or a tablet."

Skip cocked his head and raised an eyebrow. "I'm impressed, Dan the Man. That's pretty technical, for you. A few months ago you barely knew how to use a smart phone."

"Yeah, well, I figured it out," Dan said proudly.

"Maxine told him about it and showed him how to stream the video," Mel said.

Dan shot Mel a look. "I could have figured it out on my own," he snapped back.

"I know you could," Mel said condescendingly.

"Anyway," said Dan. "When the killers—I mean thieves—show up, we'll rush in."

Skip threw up his arms. "Whoa, Dan the Man! What do you mean killers?"

"I meant thieves," Dan said.

"But you said *killers*."

"The two guys who stole the money also killed at least four people that we know of," said Mel. "Maybe even two others."

"Thanks, Mel," Dan said.

"Yeah, thanks, Mel" Skip said. "Were you just gonna leave the killer part out?"

"I would have told ya."

"When?"

"Probably tomorrow."

"Probably, dude?"

"Everything will be fine," Dan said. "Trust me."

"Trust you? Last time I trusted you, a man by the name of Omar Wheeler tried to bash my skull in with a gun and I laid in the bushes unconscious for an hour, bleeding to death."

"Come on. Bleeding to death? You're over-exaggerating a little, don't ya think?"

Skip pointed to the back of his head. "Twenty-eight stitches!" he bellowed.

"Calm down, calm down. We're gonna head out. We'll be back in the morning around seven."

"Should I go ahead and put some price tags on some things?" Skip asked.

Dan shrugged. "Sure, go ahead."

Dan and Mel got up from the table. Mel walked over and put his hand on Skip's back. "Don't worry, pal, we won't let the killers kill you," he said, planting an affectionate peck on Skip's blond head.

"Thanks, Melinator," Skip said. "I really appreciate that."

As Dan and Mel were climbing back into the bug, Mel looked across the top of the vehicle at his best friend.

"Hey, Dan," Mel said.

"Yeah, Mel?" Dan replied.

"You think from now on *you* could call me the Melinator? I kind of like that."

Dan pondered the request for just a second. "No. How about if I call you the Mel-*anoma*?"

"Isn't that like a mole or something?"

"Yeah, but it's a special kind of mole. You know, like you're a special kinda person."

Mel smiled. "Thanks, Dan."

"You're welcome, pal."

Chapter Twenty-One

At three-thirty that afternoon Maxine arrived from work at Dan's place. Dan was sitting in his recliner in front of the television and Mel was in the guest room taking a nap.

"Wow," Maxine said as she entered the house. "It's quiet in here. Not used to that."

Dan took a sip of the tequila, Seven, and lime he had balanced on the arm of the chair. "This is how it used to always be," he commented.

Maxine tossed her car keys on the small table next to Buddy's bed. "And then me and Mel came along."

"And filled my days with fun and excitement. Wouldn't have it any other way."

Maxine said, "I love you," as she walked by on her way to the kitchen.

"Who wouldn't?" Dan replied. He watched Maxine's ass as she made her way across the floor. When she disappeared into the kitchen his eyes went back to *The Rifleman.*

"This coffee still from this morning?" Maxine called out.

"Yut." Dan heard the cupboard door open and then shut, then the same for the microwave oven, and finally the *ding* telling him the coffee was hot.

"Mel napping?" she asked, as she returned to the living room.

"Yut."

She grabbed a dining room chair and dragged it over in front of the TV.

"You want to sit here?" Dan asked.

"No, I'm gonna drink this cup of coffee and then jump in the shower."

"You hungry?"

"I'm getting there. We'll grab something while we're out."

Dan made a face. "Out? Out where?"

"I thought this afternoon would be a good time to start round two of the furniture shopping."

"I thought we were done with that."

"We're not done till you have furniture."

"I have furniture."

"We're not having this discussion again." She blew into her coffee and then took a sip. "What are you watching?"

"The Rifleman."

"Never call Lucas a sod buster."

"You're learning."

Maxine's cell phone rang and she reached into her breast pocket. "Hello?"

Dan turned down the volume.

"Is everything okay?" Maxine asked.

"Who is it?" Dan asked.

Maxine ignored him. "We were going furniture shopping and then grabbing something to eat."

"Who is it?" Dan asked again.

"Just Me, Mel, and Dan," said Maxine. "Sure." She glanced at her wrist watch. "We'll pick you up in about forty-five minutes ... bye."

Maxine slid her phone back into her pocket.

"Who was that?" Dan asked.

"Kendra," Maxine replied.

"Everything okay?"

"Yeah."

"What did she want?"

"She asked what we were doing. I told her we were going to look at furniture. She asked if she could come along. I said sure."

"Why would she want to hang around with us?"

"I didn't ask."

"That douche Preston Harvey ain't coming, is he?"

"No."

"Huh. Twenty-three-year-old single girl in Key West, and she wants to tag along to a furniture store. You would think she would want to go to the beach or hit some bars, or go shopping."

"Maybe she likes being around us."

"Because we're so much fun?" Dan asked.

"Maybe because we're *not* so much fun."

"Speak for yourself." Dan turned the volume back to where it was.

Maxine downed the last of her coffee, set the cup on the dining room table and headed for the bedroom. "You give Mel his medication today?"

"Yut."

"Morning and afternoon?"

"Yut."

Maxine paused at the entrance to the hall. "So, everything went good today?"

"Yeah, but if he mentions anything to you about ear pills, I have no idea what he's talking about."

"Huh, that's weird. He's never been on any medication for his ears."

Dan put up his hands. "I don't know. Crazy people, right? What are ya gonna do?"

"I ask myself that every day."

Chapter Twenty-Two

Dan pulled into the circle in front of the Atlantic Inn and was swiftly met by Billy Denton, one of the valets. Dan rolled down the window of the Ford Focus.

"Oh, hey, Mr. Coast," Billy said.

"It's just Dan, Billy and we're not staying. Just picking someone up."

"Ms. Hunt?" Billy asked.

"Yes."

Billy smiled and his face reddened a little. "Nice girl," he said.

Dan grinned. "Nice girl, Billy? She's a year older than you."

"Um ... yeah, I know." His face darkened two more shades. "I spoke with her earlier this morning, after her run." He backed away from the car. "I'll let you roll up that window, Mr. Coast, it's hot out here."

"Stay hydrated, Billy!" Mel shouted from the back seat.

Dan rolled up the window and turned around to Mel. "Stay hydrated?"

"It's hot out there," said Mel.

Maxine watched as Billy walked back behind the podium. "Looks like someone might have a crush on little Ms. Hunt," she pointed out.

"Looks that way," Dan agreed.

"No I don't," said Mel.

Dan shook his head. "We're not talking about you, Mel."

"I was gonna say, she's a little young for me." After a pause he added, "But she did suck my finger, though. Just like it was a lollipop."

Maxine whirled around to look at him. "She sucked your *what*?"

"Oh, Christ," Dan moaned. "I'll tell you later."

At that moment the doors parted and out walked Kendra. She was wearing a white sleeveless sun dress with spaghetti straps and red and yellow flowered print. She wore red Polo sneakers and carried a small white clutch. She smiled and waved at the car.

"There she is," said Mel.

Dan and Maxine watched as Kendra paused at the podium and spoke to Billy. Billy said something back and Kendra smiled shyly.

Billy watched as she continued on to the car. There was a spring in her step that Dan and Maxine had not seen before. She opened the car door and climbed into the back seat behind Maxine, next to Mel.

"Billy's got a crush on you," Mel blurted out.

"Mel!" said Kendra. "He doesn't have a crush on me."

Dan put the car in gear and left the hotel.

"Well, his face gets really red when he talks about you," said Mel.

"He was talking about me?"

"Mel, that's enough," Dan said.

"Oh that's right," Mel said. "I forgot. Sorry, Dan."

"Forgot what?" Maxine asked.

"Don't tell women everything you know," Mel recited.

"Christ," Dan whispered.

Maxine let it pass but Dan knew he would be asked about it later.

"Billy said he knows you really well," Kendra said.

"He did, did he?" Dan responded.

"He said you helped him and his mom out with—"

"So where's this place?" Dan quickly interrupted.

"On Roosevelt, next to Publix," Maxine said.

Dan took a left onto Kennedy Drive.

"He said you have a lot of money," Kendra said. "He said you paid for his—"

Dan cut her off again. "Across, and down a ways from the Home Depot?" he asked.

"Yeah, that's it," said Maxine.

Kendra took the hint that time and changed the subject. "So, what type of furniture are we looking for today?" she asked.

"Living room furniture," Maxine said.

"Dan only has one chair," said Mel.

"I noticed that," Kendra said.

Dan turned right at North Roosevelt Boulevard. He steered the car into a parking space in front of Royal Furniture and shut off the engine. "Come on, kids," he said as he climbed out of the car.

The four of them walked across the parking lot and into the store.

As they walked up and down the aisles Maxine paused in front of a light brown sectional with two recliners and a built-in drink table. "Do you like this?" she asked.

"Looks okay to me," Dan said.

"You like the color?"

"I don't care."

"It's got a place to put your drink there between the two recliners."

"I see that." Dan grabbed a hold of the tag and turned it around to see the price. "Holy Christ! It's forty-two hundred dollars."

"That's not a bad price for a piece of furniture of that quality," the salesman said. His name tag read HI I'M LARRY.

Dan turned to look at the man behind him and asked, "Do you have the same thing in a lesser quality, Larry?"

The question made the salesman squint a little.

"He's joking," Maxine said to Larry.

"Is he?" Dan asked.

Larry gave a phony smile. "What exactly are we looking for today?" he asked.

Dan gazed around the showroom. "I'm looking for the bar, Larry."

"I can't help you there, sir."

"We're looking for a couch and a couple chairs," Maxine said. "Maybe even a coffee table and a couple end tables."

"We're looking for all that?" Dan asked.

"Yes," Maxine said.

"But I already have an end table and a recliner."

"They're both going."

"Going? Going where?"

"Goodwill? Salvation Army? Wherever. They won't match the new stuff."

"What the Christ," Dan said under his breath and walked on down the aisle.

"Feel free to look around, ma'am. If you have any questions just give me a holler."

"Thanks, Larry."

Dan paused to look at a sofa sleeper with a palm tree pattern. Maxine walked up next to him. "Did you hear what he called me?" she asked.

Dan shot a look in Larry's direction. "No. What did he call you?"

"He called me, ma'am," Maxine said angrily.

"So?"

"I'm not a ma'am, I'm a miss."

"What's the difference?"

"Age."

"Well, you're getting up there."

"Fuck you!"

"Whoa! Don't think I ever heard that word come out of your mouth."

"Don't think I ever heard you be that much of a dick."

Dan continued to stare at the couch. "Really? I figured by now you had heard it all."

"You have some serious issues."

"Furniture shopping is really stressful. Look how we're acting. Maybe we better get out of here."

"This is the last furniture store in town. We're not leaving here until we buy something."

"Okay." Dan looked around the store again. "Where did those two go?"

"Kendra went out to smoke a cigarette and Mel followed her."

"I like this couch," Dan informed her.

"Now we're getting somewhere."

"You think they have chairs to match?"

"I'll ask Larry." Maxine turned and headed toward her favorite salesman.

Dan and Maxine stood at the checkout counter. Larry was holding Dan's credit card in his hand and had paperwork lying in front of him.

"So, we'll deliver the sofa sleeper tomorrow afternoon between noon and three," Larry said.

"I won't be home," said Dan.

"I have tomorrow off," Maxine said.

"And the two matching chairs, along with the end tables, will arrive in two weeks. We'll give you a call when they come in to schedule delivery."

"Thank you," Maxine said.

Larry handed the Visa card back to Dan. "Here you go, sir." He tore the top copy from each of the three forms. "These are your copies, and these are mine."

"Thanks," Dan said.

On their way toward the exit Maxine said, "See that was painless."

"Really? I've never needed a drink so bad in my life." Dan opened the door and held it for Maxine.

"Thank you," Maxine said on her way out.

Dan and Maxine both scanned the parking lot for Kendra and Mel, and spotted them on a median between two rows of parked cars, near a palm tree.

Two college-aged guys stood near them. Dan and Maxine started walking toward the group. The lava rocks crunched beneath their feet as they walked on the median, past the palm trees. Each palm tree was braced with four two-by-fours. One end of the brace was fastened to the tree trunk and the other end to a wooden stake driven in the ground. Dan and Maxine stepped over the two-by-fours as they walked.

Mel had positioned himself between the two men and Kendra. Dan could tell by the looks on everyone's faces that something wasn't quite right. "Everything okay?" he asked. He put out his hand to halt Maxine and stepped in front of her.

One of the boys was skinny and dark-complected; his face was terribly pockmarked. He wore Dollar Tree's answer to Wayfarers, a black T-shirt, and old faded jeans. The other kid was shorter, rounder, and had long greasy hair. He was wearing a white wife-beater and navy-blue nylon track pants with the buttons running up the outside of each leg.

"Take off, pal," Skinny said.

"Yeah, take off," Track Pants repeated.

"Kendra, you and Maxine go wait in the car," Dan said.

Skinny moved closer to Kendra; Mel didn't budge. "She ain't goon' nowhere. Are ya, sweetheart? Not every day a couple a regular guys like us get to meet a big famous porn star."

"It's okay, Dan," Kendra said.

"Yeah, Dan, It's okay," said Track pants. "We just want her autograph. On our dicks!"

Kendra's lip curled into a snarl. "Probably only room for my initials."

Skinny guffawed. "Good one, bitch!" Mebbe we'll settle for sumpin' else. Whaddaya say, porn star, how 'bout you give us a little peek a that shaved beaver uh yours?"

Maxine tried to move forward but Dan put out his arm again to stop her.

"Yeah, ya little whore, we know what you like. We seen all your—" That was all skinny got out before Dan hit him in the side head with one of the two-by-four braces he had ripped from a tree.

As Skinny hit the ground, Mel grabbed Track Pants by the throat, lifting him into the air and slamming him on the hood of a nearby car. Mel raised his hands over his head and, interlocking his fingers, brought his fists down on the young man's nose; it exploded like a rotted tomato. Mel hit him again, and as he raised his hand up a third time Dan grabbed his arm.

"That's enough, Mel," Dan said. "I think he gets it."

Dan and Mel stepped over Skinny as they walked away.

Kendra did the same, and as she stepped over the unconscious turd lying motionless on his back, she paused, straddling him. "There's your beaver shot, asshole," and then kicked him in the ribs as hard as she could.

Chapter Twenty-Three

It was six-thirty Saturday evening by the time Dan and Maxine dropped Kendra back at the Atlantic Inn. Harvey Preston had called her at least three times during lunch wondering what time she would be back.

Dan rode the elevator with Kendra up to the seventh floor. Maxine and Mel waited in the car.

"I'm really sorry about what happened outside the furniture store," Kendra said for the fourth time that afternoon.

Dan shrugged and said, "I told you already, it's not your fault. Those guys were just a couple of assholes. It's not your fault."

"It's not just them. That's how everyone sees me—as just some little whore."

"No, it's not. That's not how Maxine and I see you."

Kendra hugged Dan and the elevator doors parted. Harvey stood in the hallway waiting for her.

"Thank you," Kendra said, and rose up on her tip-toes to kiss Dan on the cheek.

Harvey looked at his watch. "Well, it's about time," he said. "I was lucky enough to book you at the Golden Girl tonight at nine."

"Lucky me," Kendra sighed as she stepped off the elevator.

"Yeah, lucky you," Harvey said. He nodded to Dan and Dan nodded back. "I swear, this girl don't appreciate anything I do for her."

"She's lucky to have you, Harvey," Dan said.

"Thank you," said Harvey.

Dan poked his head around the corner. Kendra was almost to her room. "Hey," he said.

Kendra turned.

"If you need anything, call me," Dan said.

Kendra smiled and walked into her room.

"Thanks, Coast," Harvey said. "I'll cut you a check before we leave town. I know she fired you, but you've been a great help."

Dan hit the button to close the elevator doors. "Don't worry about it, Harvey." Dan stuck his foot between the doors to halt them and stood in the doorway, stroking his chin reflectively. "Uh, Harvey? There's something I've been wanting to say to you."

"Yeah? What?"

"Never mind. Maybe this isn't the best time."

As the elevator doors closed on Dan's brooding face, Preston Harvey felt a cold shiver run up his spine.

*****

"How did it go?" Maxine asked as Dan got back into the car.

"Fine," Dan replied.

"What did Preston say?"

"He can't figure out why she doesn't appreciate anything he does for her."

"With friends like that," said Maxine.

"Exactly."

"I could go for some ice cream," Mel said.

"Me too," Maxine agreed.

Dan pulled away from the hotel. "Me too. I wish there was such thing as alcoholic ice cream."

"There's pina colada-flavored," Maxine said.

"And I think there's rum-flavored," Mel added.

"I think I'll get peanut butter swirl," said Maxine.

"Is toot sweet a flavor?" Mel asked.

"No," Dan replied.

"It sounds like a flavor."

"Well, it's not."

"Well, it should be."

Chapter Twenty-Four

Maxine rolled over in bed. "What time is it?" she yawned.

Dan sat at the edge of the mattress stretching his arms above his head. "Six," he replied.

"You sure get up early nowadays. Going running again?"

He grabbed his boxer shorts that lay on the floor next to his feet and slid them on. "No, gotta get over to Skip's—his moving sale starts today."

"He's moving?" Maxine rubbed the last seven hours from her eyes with the tips of her fingers. "Oh, the *pretend* moving sale."

"Yeah." Dan got up and headed for the bathroom.

"So, you went with my idea."

He paused at the door and looked back over his shoulder. "Your idea," he mumbled, and went on.

"You want me to make you some breakfast?" she called out.

"Sure, that would be great," he said and shut the bathroom door behind him.

Maxine threw back the covers and let out a loud sigh. "Coming right up."

Mel was sitting in Dan's recliner watching a classic episode of *Welcome Back, Kotter.* He was dressed in a pair of jeans and a gray Fruit of the Loom T-shirt. His aluminum foil-covered cardboard police badge hung from his neck.

"He up yet?" Mel asked when Maxine walked into the room.

"He's in the bathroom," Maxine answered. She paused and stared at Mel for a second. Something about him was different but she couldn't put her finger on it; she proceeded into the kitchen. "I'm making some breakfast."

"French toast?" Mel asked.

"You want French toast?"

"I love French toast."

"So, then you want French toast?"

"I'd rather have pancakes."

"Pancakes it is." Maxine filled the coffee maker's reservoir with tap water and then scooped coffee into the filter she had placed into the basket.

Mel could smell the coffee almost as soon as she removed the lid. "Can I have a cup of coffee this morning?" he asked.

"You know you're not supposed to have caffeine."

"They should make coffee without caffeine," said Mel.

"They do, Mel."

"You're just now telling me this?"

"I assumed you knew."

"Will you get some for next time I'm here?"

"Sure."

Mel stared at the television. "When do I have to go back to the loony bin?" he asked.

Maxine stuck her head into the room. "Loony bin?"

"That's what Dan calls it."

Maxine shook her head. "Dan's an idiot."

"You see it too?"

"Everyone sees it, Mel." She went back to making breakfast.

The bathroom door opened and Dan walked from the hallway into the dining room. He was still wearing only his boxers. He paused and stared at Mel. "What are you doing up already?" he asked.

"I couldn't sleep. I was too excited about catching the bad guys today."

"We don't know if we'll be catching any bad guys today," Dan said. He turned his head toward the kitchen and announced a little louder, "It's not that great of a plan. It probably won't even work."

"Because you didn't think of it," Maxine hollered back.

Mel's attention returned to the television.

"There's something different about you this morning," Dan observed.

"I shaved my mustache," Mel said, not looking away from the TV.

Dan scratched his head. "Oh yeah. You look better without."

"Younger?" Mel asked.

"No," Dan replied. "Just less like a pedophile."

"Thanks," Mel said.

Dan went toward the kitchen for a cup of coffee. "You're welcome."

"Quit picking on him," Maxine said.

"I wasn't picking on him," Dan responded.

"You always pick on him."

"He picks on *me*." Dan poured his coffee and took a sip. "Pancakes?"

"Yeah, Mel asked for pancakes."

"I was hoping for French toast."

"Mel asked first."

"Where's the dog?"

"Probably next door."

Dan opened the back door and looked around the yard and then whistled for Buddy. He stuck his head out and looked toward Bev's house. "Yeah, he's over there." Dan stepped out onto the steps and whistled again. Buddy lifted his head, saw it was Dan, and dropped his head to the deck again. "Should have sent that damn dog to some kind of obedience school."

Standing at the stove, Maxine moistened her lips, put her pinky and thumb between her lips leaving a slight gap, and let out a loud, shrill whistle. Buddy jumped to his feet and ran to the house.

"Show-off," said Dan.

Buddy walked right past Dan and up to Maxine. He pushed his head against her leg. She reached down and patted him on the head. "Good boy," she said.

"Yeah, good boy," Dan said. "I'll have my breakfast at the picnic table." He walked outside and let the screen door slam behind him.

Chapter Twenty-Five

Dan parked the pink Volkswagen Bug around the corner from Skip's house. As he and Mel walked along Seventeenth Street back toward Skip's, he spotted a 2x3-foot cardboard sign in Skip's yard that read, Moving SALE: EVERYTHING MUST GO.

"What the Christ is that?" Dan asked.

"It's a sign that says moving sale," Mel answered.

Dan grabbed the sign and ripped it from the wooden stake it was fastened to on his way up the walkway to the front door.

Skip's door was unlocked; Dan went in without knocking.

"What the hell, dude?" Skip said. "You ripped my signage out of the ground. Not cool, bro."

"I doubt these guys are riding around town looking for moving sale signs," Dan informed him. "And we don't want a bunch of people just stopping in."

"Whatever, dude."

Mel looked around the kitchen at Skip's appliances, each one with its own price tag. "Wow, Skip," he said. "Only a hundred bucks for the fridge. That's a great price. I need a fridge. Dan, can I buy the fridge?"

"Oh my God!" Dan exclaimed. "It's not really for sale, Mel. He's not really selling any of his shit."

"Actually, dude," Skip cut in, "I have some stuff I wanted to get rid of and I thought this would be a good opportunity. There's a guitar and amp in the other room. Also, there's a—"

"Jesus Christ!" Dan hollered. His hands went to his head. "I hope they show up soon and shoot me in the goddamn head." He walked over and laid his camera on the counter top next to a plate of freshly baked muffins.

"Dan the Man, calm down," Skip said. "You seem a little stressed today."

"What the hell are these blueberry muffins for?" Dan asked.

"They're chocolate chip muffins, and they're for the people who show up for the sale." Skip motioned toward his Mr. Coffee. "I made coffee too."

"Great idea, Skip," Mel said.

Dan dropped his head. "I need some air." He went out the back door and into Skip's yard. It wasn't even eight o'clock but Dan wanted a tequila, Seven, and lime in the worst way. He walked around the side of the house and stared out at the cars zipping by on Flagler Avenue. *I wonder where they're all going. I wish I was going with them. I need a vacation. Retirement is tough.*

Dan reentered the back door just as Red was coming in the front door. Red was carrying the microwave he had purchased on Wednesday.

"What's with the microwave?" Dan asked.

"I was gonna sell it at Skip's moving sale," Red suggested.

Dan was speechless.

"You should put a sign out front, Skip," Red said.

"Had one," said Mel.

"Dan the Man ripped it out of the ground," Skip informed him.

"I think I'm gonna have a stroke," said Dan.

"Yeah, you look a little tense, pal," Red said.

"How much you want for the microwave?" Mel asked.

"I paid forty for it ... so I'd like to get my money back."

Mel turned to Dan.

"Don't even fuckin' ask, Mel," Dan said through his clenched teeth.

"Sor-*ee*!"

"Hey!" Red said excitedly. "Are those muffins for everybody?"

"They're for the customers," Mel said.

Dan looked toward the heavens and whispered, "The customers."

Chapter Twenty-Six

Dan had set his Nikon camera on top of one of Skip's kitchen cupboards. This was the second time he had used the six thousand dollar camera since purchasing it to take pictures of an unfaithful wife. Maxine had shown him the night before how to set it up to stream wireless to a web page on the Internet. Dan, Red, and Mel could now watch and hear everything that happened in Skip's kitchen, live, as it happened. They set up a viewing location in Skip's spare bedroom. Red placed his IPad on a desk that sat against the wall that separated the bedroom from the kitchen. All four men stared at the tablet.

"I guess we're ready," Dan announced.

"Crystal clear," Skip pointed out. "How come banks and convenience stores don't have this technology?"

"Or U-Haul rental locations," Dan added.

"I can see the plate of muffins," said Mel.

"Forget about the muffins," Dan said.

"I'm hungry."

"You just ate two hours ago."

"I need a drink of water." Mel left the room and shut the door behind him.

Dan, Red, and Skip watched on the IPad as Mel entered the kitchen, walked to the cupboard, and grabbed a drinking glass. He went to the sink and filled it with water. After drinking the water and placing the empty glass in the sink his eyes went to the muffins.

"Look at him," Dan said.

"He's thinking about it," said Red.

Mel looked around to make sure he was alone in the room and then reached for a muffin.

"Leave 'em alone!" Dan shouted.

Mel jumped. "I wasn't going to eat one!" he hollered back.

"Why don't you let him have a muffin?" Skip asked.

Dan turned to Skip. "He's not supposed to eat a lot of sugar."

"One muffin ain't gonna hurt, dude."

"Okay, while we're at it," Dan said through gritted teeth, "let's give him a Mountain Dew to wash it down with, and a Red Bull chaser. Get Looney Tunes hopped up on caffeine, that's what we need!"

"I have Mountain Dew, if he wants one," said Skip innocently.

Smoke was practically coming out of Dan's ears.

Mel returned to the bedroom: his mouth was full and a melted chocolate chip was smeared across his chin.

"What's in your mouth?" Dan asked.

Mel swallowed. "Nuthin'."

"You have chocolate on your chin."

Mel wiped his chin. "No I don't. You do."

Dan rolled his eyes. "I'll make a deal with you, Mel. If you don't drive me nuts for the rest of the day, I'll buy you the guitar and amp Skip has for sale."

Mel grinned big. "It's a deal, Monty."

There was a knock at the door and all four men looked at each other as though their lottery numbers had just been called.

"We're on," Skip said, and raised his hand for a high five; only Mel obliged. He left the room and the other three's attention went to the IPad. They looked on as Skip answered the door.

Two gray-haired women apparently in their late seventies or early eighties stepped through the kitchen. To Dan, they were both dead ringers for Grandma Walton. *Maybe sisters*, he guessed

"Probably not the bad guys," said Red.

"Hold on," said Mel. "It could be a disguise."

"Guitar and amp, Mel," Dan said quietly.

"Oops." Mel pretended to zip his lips closed.

"Good morning, cute little old ladies," Skip greeted them.

"Little old ladies, my ass!" said the first one. "You're only as old as you feel, you smart-aleck hippie! Right, Mable?"

"Damn straight! We don't take any guff off of hippie boys, do we, Gladys?"

"I'll say we don't, sister!"

"I'm sorry, ladies, I didn't—"

"Is this where the moving sale is, hippie boy?" Gladys interrupted.

"Just say no, Skip," said Dan.

Skip pulled the door open all the way. "Yes, it is."

"We weren't sure," said Mable. "We didn't see a sign out front. Damn stupid of you not to have one, hippie boy."

Skip turned toward the camera and gave it an *I-told-you-so* look.

"Don't look at the camera, Skip," Dan said to himself.

Red chuckled.

Mel remained silent.

Skip waved his arm toward the freshly baked goodies. "There's fresh-baked muffins on the counter, and coffee, too, to enjoy while you browse."

"Well, thankee, hippie boy, don't mind if we do," said Mable.

"This is never gonna work," Dan said. "This is the stupidest plan ever."

The feisty sisters split a muffin and Skip poured them each a cup of coffee. "Cream or sugar, ladies?" he asked.

Dan's cell phone rang.

"What was that strange sound?" Gladys said.

Dan quickly reached for his cell.

"What's what?" Skip asked.

"I heard it too, Gladys," said Mable. "Hope you're not running one of those meth labs in the back room, hippie boy."

"Yeah," Dan said into the cell.

"Hey," Maxine said. "How's everything going?"

"I need some new friends," Dan stated.

"Ouch," said Red.

"That good, huh," Maxine said.

"The first customers just got here, two weird old lady sisters. Skip gave them muffins and coffee."

"Muffins and coffee? Skip's really putting on the ritz."

"It's a long story. A story that might end with, 'and Dan Coast put a gun to his own head.'"

"Eesh. I'll let you go. Love ya."

"Back at ya." Dan hung up his cell and then turned the volume down. "Make sure your cell phones are off," he told Red and Mel.

The rest of the morning and much of the afternoon went on the same way, and then around three o'clock a miracle happened ... Skip sold Red's microwave for fifty bucks.

Chapter Twenty-Seven

It was between six and seven that same evening when Dan and Mel returned home from Skip's. Maxine stood in the middle of the living room floor; she was on her cell phone.

"Do you want me to come over?" she asked.

Mel slammed the front door behind them.

"Who's that?" Dan asked, his face showing concern.

Maxine held up her index finger, and Dan walked on by into the kitchen.

Mel took a seat on the brand new sofa. "Nice," he said approvingly as he rubbed the palms of his hand on the cushions. He laid his head on the arm of the couch and kicked off his shoes.

"Calm down," Maxine said into the phone, "we'll be right over."

"Right over where?" Dan called out from the kitchen.

"Mel, put your shoes back on," Maxine said.

"Who was that?" Dan asked.

"I'm telling you! Jesus, give me a second. It was Kendra. She said Preston is really drunk and they've been fighting all afternoon. She said their flight leaves in a few hours and he left the hotel. She doesn't know where he is. She's really upset."

Dan poured himself half a cup of that morning's left-over coffee and downed it cold. "I figured this was coming."

"What do you mean?" Maxine asked. "Mel, get your shoes on."

"Can I stay here buy myself?" Mel asked.

"No, get your shoes on." She turned back to Dan. "What do you mean you figured this was coming?"

Dan thought back to his talk about money with Kendra on the front steps. "Just a feeling."

"PI intuition?" Mel asked.

"Get your shoes on, Mel" Dan roared, and then reached for his cell. He put the phone to his ear. "Bev? It's Dan. Can Mel stay with you for an hour or so?" He paused to wait for an answer. "Thanks." He hung up and pocketed his cell phone. "Mel, go over to Bev's … and take Buddy with you."

"Aye-aye," Mel responded with a smart salute. He slipped on his sneakers without untying them. "Come on, Buddy," he said, and slapped his thigh twice.

Buddy jumped up from his bed and followed Mel out the back door and down the steps.

"Close the back door!" Dan shouted.

Chapter Twenty-Eight

Dan pulled into the circle in front of the Atlantic Inn Hotel and he and Maxine jumped out of the Ford Focus. Dan tossed the keys to Billy.

"Hey, Mr. Coast," Billy said.

"Dan," said Dan.

The doors parted and Dan and Maxine entered the lobby. Dan looked to his right at the registration desk; he didn't recognize the woman behind the counter. He looked to his left into the bar.

"Check the bar, Maxine," Dan said. "See if Harvey is in there. Don't approach him. I'm going up to Kendra's room. If you don't see Harvey, come on up."

Maxine turned and headed toward the bar. Dan went straight ahead to the elevators.

The elevator door opened and Dan stepped out onto the seventh floor; the hallway was empty. When he reached Kendra's room, he knocked on the door, there was no answer; he knocked again.

"Who is it?" Kendra called out.

"Kendra, it's me, open the door," Dan replied.

The door opened. Kendra's eyes were bloodshot and puffy. There was a purple crescent shaped mark under her left eye. Her cheeks were red.

"Where's Harvey?" Dan asked.

"I don't know. Our flight leaves in a couple hours. I haven't heard from him in hours."

Dan stepped into the room and shut the door behind him. "What happened?"

"We got into a huge fight."

"He hit you?"

"Yes."

Dan leaned in for a closer look at her eye. "What was the fight about?"

"Money."

"Money?"

"Yeah. I asked him how much money I had."

Dan walked through the living room, through the kitchen, and to the open sliding glass door.

"He got that angry because you asked him about money?" Dan stared down at the pool five floors below.

"It started last night. I danced at the Golden Girl, and then signed autographs." Kendra sat on the sofa and pulled her legs up under her. "There were eight or nine guys there from a stag party. They gave Preston money and Preston said I had to sleep with the groom and his best man. I told him I didn't want to. He was furious with me. He told me if I didn't go back to their hotel with them, I would be sorry."

"Did you go?" Dan asked.

"No. I pretended I was going to go and then when Preston left the room I walked back here."

"When did he find out?"

"Not till this morning when the guys showed up wanting their money back."

There was a knock at the door.

"Who is it?" Kendra asked.

"It's Maxine."

Dan went to the door and let her in.

"Preston's not down there," Maxine said. "I asked the bartender, he said he left a few hours ago."

Kendra threw her arms around Maxine, and burst into tears. "I don't want to do this anymore, Maxine. I thought doing porn would be my ticket out of an ordinary life. I thought it would my springboard to Hollywood. God, how stupid I was! It's an empty, ugly, demeaning way of life. A trap. And I want out."

Maxine put her arms around the young girl and rubbed her back. "It's okay, Kendra, you don't have to do anything you don't want to do."

"Preston said he owns me. He said I have to do whatever I'm told."

Dan felt the heat in his face as his blood pressure rose. "Come on, let's get you out of here."

Next door they heard Preston Harvey's door open and then slam shut. Maxine put her finger to her lips to hush Kendra. She could feel Kendra shaking in her arms.

Harvey pounded on the door between the two rooms. "Open up, you little whore. Preston's gonna teach you a lesson." Harvey's speech was slurred. He spoke slowly and deliberately.

No one moved. They could here Preston's key as he slid it into the lock and turned the knob. He shoved the door open. He was holding a half empty bottle of Jameson Irish whiskey. He took a big swig.

"Well, if it isn't Sir Lancelot," Harvey said when he saw Dan standing in the room. "You call your protectors, did ya, you little bitch?"

Dan put up his hands. "We're leaving, Harvey, and Kendra's coming with us."

"*You're* leaving, but *she's* staying right here," Harvey argued.

"Please take me with you," Kendra pleaded. "Don't leave me here."

"We won't leave you here," Maxine assured her.

Harvey looked Maxine up and down with an evil grin as she spoke. "I could make some money off you, you sexy piece of ass," he said to Maxine. "Put that little nursing outfit of yours—"

Dan lunged at Harvey, grabbing him by the front of his shirt with both fists.

Harvey smashed the whiskey bottle against the dresser and swung it at Dan's abdomen, slicing Dan's shirt open, and cutting his stomach with the jagged bottle.

Dan winced in pain as he slung Harvey around and onto the sofa. "Get her out of here!" he hollered.

Harvey hit the arm of the sofa and flipped over it onto his back on the floor. The bottle rolled across the room.

Dan looked down at the blood trails coming from his wound. *Sonofabitch!*

Maxine and Kendra ran for the door.

Dan went at Harvey again as Harvey was clumsily climbing to his feet. Dan grabbed him by the shirt again lifting him up and tossing him back on the couch. He drew back his right fist and hit Harvey in the face as hard as he could. Then he hit him with a left. Dan yanked him off the couch and threw him to the floor and then scanned the room for the broken bottle, found it, and let go of Harvey to retrieve the bottle.

Harvey rolled over and climbed to his knees.

Dan grabbed the broken bottle.

Harvey was crawling toward the door. Dan grabbed him by the waist band and pulled him backwards across the rug. Harvey dug his nails into the carpet. Dan stood and gave him a swift kick to the ribs, flipping Harvey onto his back.

Dan straddled Harvey, sitting on his chest, and shoved the broken edge of the bottle against Harvey's neck. Harvey's eyes filled with fear, as he lay frozen on his back. Dan pushed the bottle a little harder.

"Your plane leaves in a little under two hours, Harvey. You better be on it or the next time you see me, I'll kill you."

Harvey tried to pull his head back into the floor to escape the whiskey bottle.

"You understand me?" Dan snarled. He pushed the bottle harder. Blood seeped out from around the broken glass.

Harvey did his best to shake his head yes.

"Good," Dan said. "And she better never hear from you again."

Dan tossed the bottle to the other side of the room and was about to get up when inspiration struck.

"I might not ever have the opportunity like this, Harvey, and I'm going to take advantage of it," he began. "You listening?"

Harvey feebly raised his eyebrows in reply.

"It's bad enough you hit Kendra. Real men don't do that. But you're way lower than that, Harvey. You must have the dick the size of a Vienna sausage to get your rocks off making a living exploiting young girls. Scumbags like you deserve to have their balls cut off and fed to them. Kendra's somebody's daughter. Maybe somebody's sister. Somebody's friend. She's not just a piece of meat that you put in a showcase with a price tag. She's a person, a person with feelings—"

"Nice speech, Coast," Harvey wheezed. "Tight young ass makes the world go round—always has, always will. Yeah, I ride the gravy train. So what? Get off your high horse, Coast! Who the fuck you think you are, the morality police?"

Dan held up his fists and looked from one to the other. "Yeah, Harvey, I guess I am. And now it's time for Officer Left and Officer Right to read you the riot act, ya piece of shit."

Chapter Twenty-Nine

Dan stood in his living room on his cell. He had changed into a new T-shirt, but a small amount of blood was seeping through. "Thanks, Michael, I owe you one."

"My pleasure, Daniel. Don't you worry about a thing," Michael purred. "I'm sending someone up to Ms. Hunt's room as we speak. You can stop by anytime tomorrow and pick up her things."

Dan thanked him once again and then hung up. "There, all taken care of," he said.

"If Preston didn't take all of her things with him," Maxine said.

"We'll cross that bridge when we come to it." Dan headed for the back door. "I'm gonna walk over to Bev's and let Mel know we're home. You want to come?"

"No," Maxine said. "I'm going to check on Kendra, and see how she's doing."

Dan gave her a peck on the lips. "You okay?"

Maxine smiled. "That was pretty exciting."

"Now you see why I do it."

"Scary, though."

"You did great. Maybe I'll start taking you with me instead of Red."

"I'll pass."

Dan went out the back door, into the darkness of the night, and through the back yards to Bev's house. Buddy was lying on her deck in front of the back door. "How's it going, boy?" Dan said. Buddy jumped to his feet and Dan patted him on the head.

Dan gave a quick knock and went in. "Hey, neighbor!" he called out.

Buddy lay back down

"In here," Bev returned.

The floor plan of Bev's bungalow was a mirror image of Dan's. Dan went from the kitchen into the dining room. Mel sat on the couch with his feet up on the coffee table, staring at the screen of his new cell phone. Bev sat in her recliner watching *Forensic Files*.

"How did everything go?" Dan asked.

"Good," Bev answered. She threw a thumb toward Mel. "He's not much for conversation now that he's got that that damn phone."

"You're welcome," Dan joked.

"How did everything go with Kendra?" Bev asked.

"Good, I guess. Her manager left, she stayed."

"What the hell happened to your stomach?"

Dan pulled his shirt away from the wound. "It's nothing. Just a little cut."

"Looks like more than a little cut."

"I'll have Maxine put a couple Band-Aids on it when I get home."

"What's Kendra going to do now?"

"Good question."

"You want a drink?"

Dan sat down next to Mel. "That would be fantastic," he said. He stretched his arms over his head and let out a big yawn. "I'm exhausted. I'm glad this day is coming to an end."

Bev got up and went to the kitchen to make Dan a drink.

"What's on television tonight, Mel?"

"I don't know," Mel replied, never looking up from his phone.

"Did you eat anything?"

"Uh-huh."

"What are ya playin'—Angry Birds, or some shit?"

"No."

"You're worse than a kid. Ya know that?"

Bev returned with Dan's tequila and 7Up. "Sorry, no limes."

"See if I ever drink in this bar again," Dan said, taking the glass from her.

Mel chuckled. "They're eating the muffins," he said.

"What?" Dan asked.

"The guys at Skip's house, they're eating the muffins."

"What guys?" Dan asked, and leaned closer to Mel to get a better look at his cell phone.

Mel tilted the screen toward Dan. "The two guys at Skip's house," he repeated.

"Jesus Christ!" Dan shouted. He reached in his pocket for Maxine's car keys. "Bev, I gotta go." He set his drink on the coffee table and ran for the front door, stopped, turned, and ran for the back door.

"What's the matter?" Bev shouted.

On his way out the door Dan hollered back, "Keep Mel here!"

Dan jumped over Buddy and leapt from the deck, over the steps, and into the backyard. Buddy let out a bark.

Dan ran as fast as he could to his house, yanking the screen door open when he got there. "They're at Skip's!" he shouted.

Maxine jumped up from the couch. "Who's at Skip's?"

Dan ran past her and turned down the hallway. He dropped to his knees in front of his bedroom closet, pulled back the carpeting, and removed a wooden plank in the closet floor. He reached into the dark compartment and pulled out a black duffle bag.

Maxine came into the bedroom. "What's the matter?" she asked.

"The guys who took my money, they're at Skip's house right now." He unzipped the bag, reached inside and pulled out his 9mm. He released the clip, checked its contents, and shoved it back into the grip.

"Should I call the police?" Maxine asked.

"No. I don't need them pulling in there with their goddamn lights flashing."

"What do you want me to do?"

Dan jumped to his feet, kissed Maxine. "If you don't hear from me in forty-five minutes, call Rick and tell him what happened."

"Let me call him now."

"No!"

Dan ran down the hall for the front door.

"I love you!" Maxine shouted.

It was too late, Dan was already out the door.

Chapter Thirty

Dan Coast took a left off of Flagler Avenue onto Sixteenth Street and then a quick right onto Eagle Avenue. He killed the lights and pulled to the curb. With his 9mm jammed into his waistband he ran around the corner onto Seventeenth Avenue. He ran halfway down the block and climbed, as stealthily as he could, over Skip's chain link fence, and then duck-walked up to the kitchen window. He peered through the open window. The kitchen light was on and he could see down the hallway into the living room. The living room was also lit; there was no sign of Skip or the other two men.

Dan put his ear to the screen but could hear nothing but his own breathing and heartbeat. He moved down the side of the house and to the front where he could look through the living room window. When he peeked in he saw two men walking down the hall, back toward the kitchen. Still no sign of Skip. Dan thought of his friend, dead and stuffed in the bedroom closet, like the Murphy's.

Getting down on his hands and knees and pulling the pistol from his waistband he crawled under the living room window and around to the side door. A window next to the door was open and he could now hear the two men talking; he knew that time was of the utmost importance.

"Just get in there and put a bullet in the idiot's head," one of the men said.

Dan breathed a sigh of relief. Skip wasn't dead—yet—but the lovable doofus's life hung in the balance.

"I did it last time," the other man argued.

Dan got to his feet and peered through the window. Neither man was holding a weapon but they were packing. Dan wished Red were with him. He always felt safer when the big man was near, but this couldn't wait.

Pulling the screen door open as quietly as he could he slid the holding bracket up the closer arm propping the door open. He gripped his weapon, placed his finger on the trigger, and gently pulled back the slide and pushed it back into position.

"Okay, I'll do it," the man said.

Dan took a deep breath and kicked open the door. Both men turned toward the door. Dan fired once, hitting the taller man in the shoulder and driving him back against the countertop. He trained the 9mm on the other man, who was reaching into his shoulder holster for his own weapon. Dan fired twice. With a shriek the man sprawled backwards into the cabinets, staggered drunkenly for maybe two seconds, and collapsed to his knees with twin bullet holes in his chest at nine and three o'clock.

Dan turned the weapon back to the first man and fired two more times, once into the man's chest and once into his forehead.

Both men lay dead on Skip's kitchen floor, blood pooling on the white ceramic tile.

Dan exhaled through his mouth slowly and then took another breath. He returned his gun to his waistband.

Dan dropped to his knees and felt for each man's wallet. He pulled three hundred dollars out of the shorter man's wallet and one hundred and fifty-two out of the other guy's.

"What the Christ?" he said. "Still down forty-eight bucks." He shoved the money into his pocket and went to look for Skip.

Pulling open the bi-fold door to Skip's bedroom closet, Dan gazed down at his friend, sitting on the floor, bound and gagged.

"You ready to come out of the closet?" Dan asked.

Chapter Thirty-One

The next day, Monday morning, Maxine Myers sat in one of the Adirondack chairs next to the fire pit. Kendra Hunt was seated in the other chair. Kendra was scratching Buddy's head as he lay on the ground next to her chair.

Mel was seated at the picnic table, staring into his cell phone. Dan sat *on* the picnic table with his feet on the bench.

They all turned their heads when they heard Bev call out, "Mornin' neighbors!"

Mel jumped up to grab her a lawn chair from the tool shed.

Bev carried with her a large mug of coffee. "How's everyone this morning?" she asked.

"Good," everyone replied.

"Wonderful!" Dan said.

Mel unfolded the lawn chair and placed it between Maxine and Kendra; Bev sat down and put her feet up on the fire pit. Mel returned to his seat and his eyes went back to the cell phone's screen.

They all turned toward the gravel path that led to the driveway when they heard Red holler, "Am I too late for breakfast?" He walked down the path and sat at the picnic table next to Mel.

"Can't get your nose out of that phone, can ya?" Red asked. "What are ya looking at?"

"Skip's mopping his floor," Mel replied.

Red leaned in for a closer look. "What the hell did he spill? Is that wine or Kool-Aid, or something—"

"It's blood," said Mel matter-of-factly.

"Blood?"

"Yeah, Dan shot two guys last night."

"What! What do you mean, shot two guys?"

"It's pretty self-explanatory," Dan said.

"Who did you shoot?" Red asked.

"The two guys we were looking for showed up at Skip's last night."

Red looked to the ladies. "Is he serious?"

They all nodded yes.

"We watched the whole thing on Mel's phone," said Bev.

Mel chuckled. "Look, Skip's picking his nose."

"We even watched him steal their money after he shot them," Maxine said disgustedly.

"So, you got your money back," Red said.

"No. Would you believe Rick made me give it back?"

"How do you give money back to dead people?" Red asked.

"I had to give it to Rick," Dan answered. "Evidently it's evidence."

"That sucks."

"Tell me about it. This week I got in two fights, a shootout, got my stomach slashed, and solved four murders—"

"Six, counting the couple in Allentown," Maxine added.

"That's right, six. All that and it ended up *costing* me five hundred bucks."

"Poor baby," said Maxine.

"There's just not a lot of money in crime-solving," Dan said.

"That's why Rockford lived in a trailer," Mel said.

"And Magnum lived in a guest house," said Red.

"And Rod Hardman lived in his van," Kendra said.

Everyone looked at Kendra confusedly.

"No one?" she asked. "No one has seen Rod Hardman, PI?"

"No," Maxine said.

"Huh. I played a nurse in that one."

The End

Coming 2017

Sunrise City

Also by Rodney Riesel

Sleeping Dogs Lie
From the Tales of Dan Coast

A mystery set in the Florida Keys follows Dan Coast, an unlicensed private detective of sorts, as he is hired to find the missing boyfriend of a woman who herself soon ends up missing. When someone from the woman's past unexpectedly shows up at Dan's home, with a story of faked deaths and missing life insurance money; Dan along with his sidekick Red set out to find the money, and the woman.

ISBN: 978-0-9883503-0-4

Ocean Floors
From the Tales of Dan Coast

The second installment in the Dan Coast series, Ocean Floors, is a tale of mystery and possible romance when a chance meeting with a beautiful young woman leads Dan and his trusted sidekick Red down a road of murder and kidnapping. Join Dan and Red as they try to solve the murder while searching for a missing friend.

ISBN: 978-0-9894877-0-2

North Murder Beach
A Jake Stellar Novel

The first installment of the story of North Myrtle Beach police detective, Jake Stellar. The spring bike rallies have ended, the spring breakers have all gone back to school, and the summer tourist season is a few weeks away. What better time for a police officer to take a nice quiet relaxing week off from work? That's what Jake Stellar had in mind. That is until someone from his past resurfaces to remind him of a terrible secret he has spent years trying to forget. In North Murder Beach, a story of revenge, Jake is unwillingly and violently forced to confront his secret from his past.

ISBN: 978-0-9894877-1-9

The Coast of Christmas Past
From the Tales of Dan Coast

Coast of Christmas Past is the third book in the Dan Coast series of books. Dan Coast is all set to spend Christmas just the same way he has every year for the past few years; alone and drunk. But when uninvited, unexpected guests arrive and throw a wrench into his holiday plans he is forced to sober up (slightly), and throw on a smile. Just when it seems nothing else could go wrong, a close friend is injured in what appears, to the police, to be a drug deal gone bad. Dan Coast and his sidekick, Red jump into action to find the truth while their friend lies unconscious in the hospital.

ISBN: 978-0-9894877-3-3

The Man in Room Number Four
The Dunquin Cove Series

When a mysterious stranger arrives in the small coastal town of Dunquin Cove, Maine it appears as though Claire and her young son, Mica's prayers have been answer.

But who is he, and why is he really here? Join Claire and her guests at the Colsome House Bed and Breakfast as they piece together the mystery of the Man in Room Number Four.

ISBN: 978-0-9894877-2-6

Ship of Fools
From the Tales of Dan Coast

Ship of Fools is the fourth book in The Tales of Dan Coast series and begins where Coasts of Christmas Past left off. Find out how Dan deals with the death of a young friend, while looking into the disappearance of a new friend's sister. Join Dan, Red, and Skip as they fumble their way through a new mystery.

ISBN: 978-0-9894877-4-0

Beach Shoot
A Jake Stellar Series

It's a beautiful Sunday morning in North Myrtle Beach and Emily Bowen, a wife and mother of four, lies dying on the beach. Jake Stellar returns in Beach Shoot, a new mystery by Rodney Riesel.

Beach Shoot is the second Jake Stellar book and sequel to the Amazon Best Seller North Murder Beach. In Beach Shoot, Jake finds himself teamed up with the most unlikely of partners, his nemesis and fellow detective Avis Lint. Join Jake and Avis as they piece together the clues in this thrilling new mystery.

ISBN: 978-0-9894877-5-7

Return to Dunquin Cove
The Dunquin Cove Series

It's been almost six months since the day ex-hitman, Ben Dunning turned up in Dunquin Cove, Maine, not knowing where or who he was. He's lived a quiet, peaceful life in the small town, but now his old life is calling him back. As Ben plans a trip to Boston in search of his past, little does he know that trouble is brewing in Dunquin Cove. Two strangers have arrived with the promise of safety and security. Join Ben and the people of Dunquin Cove as they band together to prove they can take care of themselves and their town.

ISBN: 978-0-9894877-7-1

Double Trouble
From the Tales of Dan Coast

Shortly after Walter and Warren Bowman arrive in Key West in search of a sister they never knew they had, Warren disappears. With nowhere else to turn, Walter enlists the help of Dan Coast. Join Dan as he and sidekick Red Baxter search for the missing Bowman family members, while dealing with the fallout of an ongoing case.

ISBN: 978-0-9894877-9-5

When Death Returns
A Jake Stellar Series

Has a serial killer from the past returned to North Myrtle Beach? Jake Stellar is back in When Death Returns. Join Jake and his partner Avis Lint in this exciting third installment of the Jake Stellar series as they investigate a homicide that eerily echoes the past.

ISBN: 978-0-9971149-0-4

From Here to There: A Collection of Short Stories

Within this book is a collection of short stories I have written over the past few years. The stories were mostly inspired by trips I've taken, places I've stayed, and conversations I've overheard from Maine to Florida. Although these stories differ from ones I have released in the past, I hope you will enjoy reading them as much as I enjoyed writing them.

ISBN: 978-0-9971149-1-1

Most Likely to Die
From the Tales of Dan Coast

How does someone with no enemies end up murdered? That's for Dan Coast and his sidekick Red Baxter to find out. Join Dan and Red, along with Skip Stoner and Dan's childhood hero, former astronaut, Kip Larson as they piece together the clues that may free an innocent man. In this action packed, sixth installment of The Tales of Dan Coast Series, Dan digs into a wrongly accused man's past and finds out he may not be so innocent.

ISBN: 978-0-9971149-2-8

The Obedience of Fools
A Jake Stellar Series

Join Detective Jake Stellar and his partner, Detective Avis Lint in this fast paced, North Myrtle Beach based Jake Stellar Series. In this fourth installment, The Obedience of Fools, Jake and Avis butt heads with some of The Grand Strand's elite as they try to uncover a secret that may hold the answer to a string of recent homicides.

ISBN: 978-0-9971149-3-5